In the Snowbird Mountains
and Other Stories

Also by Robert Morgan

FICTION

The Blue Valleys
The Mountains Won't Remember Us
The Hinterlands
The Truest Pleasure
Gap Creek
The Balm of Gilead Tree: New and Selected Stories
This Rock
Brave Enemies
The Road From Gap Creek
Chasing the North Star
As Rain Turns to Snow

NONFICTION

Good Measure: Essays, Interviews, and Notes on Poetry
Boone: A Biography
*Lions of the West: Heroes and Villains of the Westward
   Expansion*

POETRY

Zirconia Poems
Red Owl: Poems
Land Diving: Poems
Trunk & Thicket
Groundwork
Bronze Age
At the Edge of the Orchard Country
Sigodlin: Poems
Green River: New and Selected Poems
Wild Peavines: New Poems
Topsoil Road
The Strange Attractor: New and Selected Poems
October Crossing
Terroir
Dark Energy: Poems
*The Oratorio That Was Time: Fourteen Poems and Three
   Stories*

IN THE
SNOWBIRD
MOUNTAINS
AND OTHER STORIES

ROBERT MORGAN

Press 53
Winston-Salem

Press 53, LLC
PO Box 30314
Winston-Salem, NC 27130

First Edition

Cover photograph, "Rabbit Hole,"
Copyright © 2016 by nadiasphoto
licensed through iStock Photo

Author photo by Robyn Wishna

Cover design by Kevin Morgan Watson & Claire V. Foxx

Library of Congress Control Number
2023930519

ISBN 978-1-950413-63-8

For Jesse Graves and Randall Wilhelm

CONTENTS

The Body on Mt. Mitchell   1

The Wonderful City   15

Devil's Courthouse   35

Beyond the Outer Banks   59

Judaculla Rock   85

The Secret Face   103

In the Snowbird Mountains   117

Hurricane   139

Acknowledgments   177

Author Biography   179

THE BODY ON MT. MITCHELL

When the body of Prof. Elisha Mitchell was found in a pool below a waterfall in 1857, the cold water had preserved the corpse remarkably well. His blue eyes stared at the peak above whose height he'd measured and which would be named for him. The summit, 6,684 feet above sea level, would be declared the highest east of the Mississippi. The professor from Chapel Hill had been on another expedition to explore the mountain, and on June 27, 1857, caught by night, apparently stumbled over the rim of the falls to his death. For more than a week no one knew what had happened, until his son Charles, with the aid of the bear hunter Big Tom Wilson and others, scoured the thickets and lower slopes and discovered the body. They even found at the bottom of the pool the barometer used to gauge elevation.

As the editor of a small-town paper in piedmont North Carolina, fighting for its life in the age of television and social media, I thought it would be an excellent idea to

combine recreation with work and follow Prof. Mitchell's footsteps, starting from the scene of his death and
climbing to the peak, making notes and taking pictures
of the hollows and ridges as I went. I wanted to write
a feature on Mitchell, the history of exploration of the
Black Mountains, and the conditions of the region today. Perhaps I might see Mitchell's ghost. To keep me
company, I brought my miniature collie Wallie, short for
William Wallace.

I'd grown up in the mountains of North Carolina,
before the region was overrun by tourists and retirees.
It was always a delight to return there, especially in
summer, to escape the furnace of the Piedmont. The
blue wall of mountains loomed so cool as I approached
on the Interstate that my eyes grew damp. The breeze
on those ridges was better than air conditioning.

The waterfall where Elisha Mitchell died was on
Cane River, but the exact location didn't appear on
any map, not even the Geological Survey maps of the
mountain chain. I told myself that was good: I would
have the excitement of searching for the site. Readers
enjoy accounts of hardships overcome, from the
comfort of their armchairs.

To reach the skirts of Mt. Mitchell, I turned onto
Highway 221 and wound up to the Blue Ridge Parkway.
My hope was to stop at one of the scenic overlooks.
Whether overnight parking was permitted along the
road, I didn't know; if no signs forbade it, I would be
bold. The lot I chose was just under the soaring shoulder
of the famed peak. Wallie was happy as I was to get
out of the car and find our hiking legs. I grabbed my
backpack and was about to lock the car when a ranger
SUV drove up. The patrolman was a young man wearing
aviator sunglasses, friendly, but the revolver on his hip
reinforced the uniform's authority.

"We encourage people to hike on marked trails," he
said.

I explained I was researching a story on Prof. Mitchell

and the state park and its maintenance. How could I write about the mountain unless I explored close-up some of the hidden hollows few tourists saw? It was the mention of the park and its maintenance that seemed to have the right effect. I took out my phone and clicked a picture of him beside the SUV.

"Start no fires and damage no wildlife," the ranger warned. "If you're injured off the trails that's your sole responsibility." I assured him no theft or injury would be blamed on the Park Administration. Then he drove away so he could claim he never saw me enter the woods with a backpack, and therefore had not failed in his duty. I wished I'd asked the exact location of the waterfall where Prof. Mitchell had fallen.

After driving for hours, both Wallie and I walked awkwardly. On a steep slope you tend to stumble anyway. In the balsam thickets you have to stoop under limbs and thread your way between trees. The backpack got in the way. Twigs stung my face and cobwebs stretched over my eyes and stuck to my cap. Wallie had it easier, closer to the ground, running ahead, circling back, whimpering, ecstatic to be on an adventure. The mountain air was fresh.

After struggling through fir trees and spruces I reached a rhododendron thicket, what was called by local people a "laurel slick." That was easier going than through the balsams.

It was getting toward late afternoon, and I was tired. I thought of battling my way back to the car and finding a motel, but then realized I'd left the rhododendrons behind. The woods were more open, and the trees mostly beech and oak. Walking now would be simpler. I just had to find a stream to camp by. Wallie sprinted forward and back, his curiosity and energy boundless.

The only stream I found was a branch that splashed in steps from rock to rock. The ground was just level enough to spread my sleeping bag with the head uphill. I cleared a patch of twigs, leaves, and litter to start a small fire to warm rice and roast wieners, make instant coffee. I gave Wallie some wieners and dog chow. After the grub and coffee, things looked better. While light lingered, I took out a notebook and recorded the day's activities, including the frustration of contending with the balsam thicket and rhododendrons.

Later, as the night cooled, I lay in the sleeping bag and watched stars through trees. Nothing will make you as calm as thinking about the great distances and silences to stars and between the stars, and galaxies flying away from us, and from each other, as though rebelling against any unity in creation. Watch out for those deep thoughts, I said. Next thing you'll be sounding like a philosopher.

I watched the coals fade into darkness, hoping the ranger hadn't spotted the flames, then floated into sleep, dreaming of a waterfall and a body drifting in the catchment basin staring at stars. I'm not sure when I realized Wallie had disappeared. At some point I heard a braying like a bull or volunteer fire department horn. In the early light, in the breeze before any redness appears in the east, I became aware that Wallie had not returned.

At first, I assumed the dog was still hunting. But more awake, I realized it was strange he'd not reappeared. I rose and called. The only answers were birds in the trees and cicadas further down the slope. What could be a threat to a dog in the forest: bears, panthers? That was most unlikely. It was known coyotes brought down dogs and cats. I pulled on my boots and looked around the campsite.

"Wallie!" I yelled between my hands. The only responses were birds and the musical chatter of squirrels and the branch tumbling over rocks. I walked down the slope along the stream and called again.

Dreading to fight my way uphill, into the thickets, I climbed back to the edge of the laurels and shouted, then stopped to listen. There was a rustle in the leaves above. I called again and again and waited. The snapping twigs and swishing of limbs drew closer, sounds of something bigger than Wallie.

"Wallie!" I shouted, and, as the rustling grew near, I instinctively backed away and tripped on a rock. Whirling to pull myself up, I saw the Park ranger of the afternoon before. "My dog is lost," I blurted. He looked at me hard. The tag on his jacket said Gus Wilson.

"Your fire was spotted last night," he said.

"It was a small fire, like the Indians made."

"I'm writing you a ticket," he said, "for parking overnight in the Park, and for building a fire in the preserve." He asked to see my driver's license.

"How much do I owe?" I said, with ice in my voice. He must have thought I was attempting to bribe him.

"You will pay at Park Headquarters, or we'll take you to court." He scribbled a ticket on his pad and handed it to me, then turned to leave.

"Wait," I said, almost shouting. He stopped and looked back. "Are you related to Big Tom Wilson, the bear hunter?"

He didn't answer for several seconds. "Why do you want to know?"

"Because I'm writing the story about Elisha Mitchell and Big Tom Wilson, who found the body."

"Mister, you have broke the law," Gus Wilson said, but he didn't walk away.

"I know I have, but I just want to get my story, to find the death falls, and remind people of the history of Mt. Mitchell."

The ranger stared, right hand resting on the revolver.

"And I must find my dog," I added.

"The falls you're looking for are a mile down the slope, bearing to your left," he said. "But you must return to your car, and if you start another fire I'll have to arrest you."

"Thank you."

"But I don't know where your dog is," Gus Wilson said before stepping into the rhododendrons.

I'd bruised my elbow when I fell, and rubbed the bone, waiting until the ranger was out of hearing before calling again.

Since Wallie didn't seem nearby, I rolled up the sleeping bag and loaded the backpack. Might as well head in the direction the ranger had indicated. At least I could tell my readers I'd found the deadly waterfall. Calling Wallie every few minutes, I descended through the hardwoods. A deer spooked and dolphined into undergrowth. Deer had been scarce in the mountains when I was growing up, but there had been a resurgence, as the fashion for hunting waned.

When I'd gone a mile and not found the waterfall, I decided I must have veered in the wrong tack. Either the waterfall was further away, or my aim had been off. The only noise was the love calls of cicadas.

"Wallie!" I shouted.

Further on, as the ground flattened, I found a curious trail in the leaves. It looked as though someone had dragged a log or heavy limb along the ground. Following the trail, I noticed tracks on either side of the trace, unlike any I'd ever seen, with four sharp toes, all about the same length, digging into dirt, heels lightly imprinting the ground. I followed the trail, mystified.

A bear paw has five toes spread in an arc. A panther has four toes in a half circle, with a deep heel print. A coyote print is much like a dog's. What kind of animal would drag itself, leaving such a trail in leaves?

The path led to a cluster of boulders. As I approached the outcrop, it occurred to me where I'd seen such four-toed prints before. Once when we took the children to Florida, at a roadside zoo, one of the exhibits was a fenced-off pen of alligators in mud and water. The gators made tracks in the mud just like those here.

The American alligator, *Alligator Mississippiensis*, had a range from the swamps of eastern North Carolina to Florida, and west to the Rio Grande. No one I knew of had ever found a gator in the Piedmont of Carolina, much less in the mountains. Alligators need water, and are allergic to cold weather. At one time they'd been declared an endangered species, but word was they'd come back in Florida with a vengeance. Yet it was unthinkable that an alligator could be found alive in the Black Mountains, at the foot of Mt. Mitchell.

That's when I remembered Wallie. Alligators were known to have a taste for small animals and birds like ducks. Stepping between the rocks, I saw more boulders surrounding a hole four or five feet across. The smell rising from the opening was too foul and repugnant to describe, an ancient scent of swamps and rotting things. I eased closer and peered over the rim. The dirt around the pit was stamped with tracks. I hesitated to glimpse inside, fearing the toothy smile of a giant lizard.

Forcing myself to look, all I found was black water surrounded by darkness. The stench was unbearable. Stepping back to breathe fresh air, I pulled the flashlight from my backpack. Shuddering to think of Willie's fate, I waited a few minutes before daring to peek again into the fetid sinkhole.

"Wallie!" I called, and shone the light on the foul water. There was only darkness, and fumes of acrid filth and decay. I thought I caught a ripple on the surface, as if something had stirred below. Bubbles rose into the light, as though gas leaked from the earth, or something breathed.

I held my breath, and pulled back to gulp the fresh breeze. Outside the cluster of boulders the air was clean and charged with oxygen. I'd never appreciated pure air so much.

It was impossible for an alligator to live in the mountains of North Carolina. The winters were much too cold, and streams too fast and icy. The land was too dry, far from swamps and dreamy, black rivers of the Coastal Plain. Everyone knew the legend of alligators in the sewers of New York City, descended from pets escaped from cages and crawling down storm drains.

It was true that deep down the earth was warm. If an alligator found its way there it might survive, for a while, if it could find something to eat. Could a family in Asheville, or nearby, with an alligator that outgrew its cage, have released the pet in the woods?

I was pondering the question when the roar of a motor approached. It was Gus the ranger on an all-terrain four-wheeler. He killed the motor.

"Mr. Williams, you must return to your car."

"I think my dog has been attacked," I said.

The ranger gave me the look he used, along with his uniform and pistol, to intimidate tourists who speeded on the access road. "What could have attacked it?" he said.

"You won't believe this." I said.

"Probably not."

"An alligator."

Gus snorted and began writing another ticket.

I showed him the prints in the leaves and around the pit among the boulders.

"You be gone before dark," he said. "Otherwise I'll have to arrest you." He handed me the second ticket. "For refusing to leave this morning it will cost you three hundred dollars," he added, then climbed back on the four-wheeler and roared away, tearing up ground and leaving a phantom of exhaust in the air.

I slid the ticket in my pocket. I'd hoped for a surprise in my story about following the steps of Prof. Mitchell, but not this kind of shock. It would be dark before I could reach my car, and I couldn't leave the site. It wouldn't be fair to Wallie to just give up.

With my hunting knife I cut a sapling about two inches thick and sharpened the end to make a spear or pike. I recalled that alligators fought with rows of razor teeth and the lash of a powerful tail. All I had besides the hunting knife were my hands and the stout pike, weapons my ancestors had relied on for tens of thousands of years.

I moved back in the trees about half a mile before unrolling the sleeping bag on a bed of moss, too tired to start a fire, even if I'd dared. I munched granola bars and drank from a nearby spring, and peeled an apple from my pack.

That night I dreamed of giant albino snakes that never saw the light of day, fish with no eyes in lightless caverns. Once, I woke and knew I'd heard an unusual sound. Katydids chanted down the slope, and their kin from the left answered, but it was not katydids that woke me.

Then it came again, sometime later, a roar or a bellow, a howl that seemed to echo from inside the mountain. Yet it sounded familiar, as if remembered from an age of steaming mires and morass and giant vegetation, when the stars were fixed in different zodiacs.

With the pike beside the sleeping bag and hunting knife by my head, I listened for the bawl, but it didn't come again. As I finally slid into sleep I wondered if the threatening cry was just a dream.

In early light I heard only birds and the chatter of a squirrel, and ate more energy bars, drank from the spring. Should I continue to search for Wallie, or hurry back to the car with my tickets before Gus came to arrest me? Was there really an alligator in this unlikely place, or had I fantasized the fate of my beloved dog? The wise thing would be to leave, but I couldn't go without more effort on behalf of Wallie.

In the gray light I scribbled a few notes about the day before, about my fear, and decision to defy the ranger and his ticket pad. I laughed, imagining Gus as a waiter taking my order for some grotesque adventure.

Rolling up the bag, shouldering the backpack, knife on my belt, I took up the pike and headed toward the outcrop of boulders. The ordinary sounds of the forest suggested I'd imagined the alligator in the hole. Maybe it was all hallucination, caused by worry about Wallie.

I was about a hundred yards from the boulders when

I spotted a fresh trail in the leaves. The trace led away from my camping spot. Something heavy had been dragged over the forest floor. If it had been a hallucination before, I was hallucinating again. Something stirred in the forest litter ahead. Early sun threw spots in pied shapes on the motley leaves. As I looked closer, I saw there *was* an alligator, materializing out of shadows.

The prehistoric animal took a step toward me, its eyes raised like frog eyes. What could I prove, confronting this demon from the age of the dinosaurs, from the era of volcanoes and flying reptiles, before there was warm blood? Raised on its two front legs, the dragon was knee high. Its tail stretched into shadows.

Common sense told me to run, to put distance between myself and this freak from extinct ages. I didn't know how quick it could dash in pursuit of prey, but I knew a lizard could whip forward like lightning. Besides the saw teeth, it had the deadly tail to lash and stun, knocking victims unconscious. On television I'd seen men wrestling alligators, but I was not one of those men.

Even as I prepared to run, the thought of Wallie forced me to hold back. The abominable lizard had devoured my loved pet, broken his bones with those terrible jaws. I gripped the spear and stepped toward the murderer.

I'm almost ashamed to confess it, but in that instant, the thought flashed through my mind of a headline, "Editor Confronts Giant Alligator For Revenge." Even in the moment of danger, I was hungry for headlines, a peddler of sensation.

As I eased forward, the gator held its ground, as though daring me. It was probably not used to seeing humans. Its eyes seemed the size of paperweights. The jaws threatened, but the tail even more. If it opened its jaws I would drive the pike down its long, wrinkled throat. Even as I edged closer, I knew it was foolish to confront the swamp goliath, but I owed it to Wallie, and maybe to children roving in the woods.

I was within ten feet, waiting for it to pounce, before

I saw the tail stretched in the undergrowth, six or eight feet long. It didn't move, and I stepped closer, raising the pike, and just at that instant the alligator turned away, as if to head back to the lair in the rocks. I impelled the shaft into one of the eyes. The gator whirled, knocking the pike loose, and opening the horrible jaws. With both hands I drove the lance into the throat as far as it would go. I put all my weight on the shaft and sank it deeper. The gator gave a kind of cough, and it seemed the pike had touched something vital.

Concentrating on my weapon, I didn't notice the tail swing round until it hit my hip. The tail was saw-like, raking my flesh and bones. I would have fallen, except I was hanging onto the pike. My thigh burned like a blowtorch was held on it. But the spear was deep inside the throat. To gag out the pike, the alligator thrashed from side to the side. I clutched the pole, flung left and right.

Again, I didn't see the tail until it struck my right leg below the knee, causing sickening pain. Even so, I gripped the pike, weak from agony and the stench of the animal's breath, as the alligator gasped and whipped its head. Whatever was festering in its guts boiled up as the alligator gulped and writhed.

In the heat of pain, I tried to keep feet on the ground, weight on the pole, but the fiend's strength and endurance were far too much for me. After one mighty jerk of the gator's head, I lost my hold and fell. The alligator would have bitten me, except the pike prevented the jaws from closing. Still, there was the tail. I rolled away as far as I could.

Someone stood just a few yards away. Gus the Park ranger looked on with astonishment, at me, and the alligator trying frantically to heave the pike out of its throat.

"Shoot it!" I screamed. "Shoot the son of a bitch!"

"We're forbidden to kill animals in the State Park."

"Does this look like an ordinary animal?"

"Where could it have come from?"

"It killed my dog."

"You're not supposed to be here," Gus snapped.

"Then let me shoot it," I said and reached for his revolver. The ranger knocked my hand away.

The alligator flung from side to side like a wounded snake, but it couldn't cough out the pike.

"Do something, you oaf!" I shouted.

Gus looked thoughtful, and then said, "I am allowed put a wounded animal out of its misery."

The ranger loosened the pistol from its holster and raised the barrel toward the alligator. When he fired two shots into the head, the animal continued to thrash, unfazed.

"Hit the heart!" I shouted, "behind the head." I thought of harpooners in *Moby Dick* taking aim.

Gus shot three more times into the knobby back near the head. The front legs gave way and the head dropped to the leaves, the pike in its throat. Its head lay still but the tail twitched and tried to swing for several minutes.

"Where did it come from?" Gus said, clearly shaken.

"Some kid probably released his pet in the wild after it grew too big to keep."

I led the ranger again to the pit between boulders and showed him the underground water that was likely not all that cold.

Inevitably, we had to discuss what to do with the body, much too heavy to carry. Gus feared he might have exceeded his authority.

"You did the only thing you could do," I assured him.

With some effort we turned the body over. Underneath, the beast was yellow-white, sectioned like tile.

"Could you cut the belly open to see if it ate my dog?" I handed him my hunting knife.

Gus looked at the carcass with leaves and litter stuck to the hide. "Are you sure you want to do that?" he said.

Gripping the knife handle with both hands, Gus ripped the belly from throat to tail. There was a lining around the cavity which he sliced and then pulled apart.

I stepped closer, and the smell almost flung me back.

It was a fetor of rotting flesh mixed with the alligator stink, diabolical, the acid of digestive juices, of meat turning to mush and excrement. Putrefying chemicals burned my face and nostrils. The end of my pike was stuck into the mess. I thought I saw hair like Wallie's, and crushed bones.

If I'd had the revolver I would have shot the murderer again.

"Mr. Williams, you'd best sit down," Gus said.

I dropped to the ground, too dazed to think. I had to blame myself for not heeding Gus's warnings. Unable to find an alternative, I did what habit dictated: grabbed the notebook from the pack and began scrawling sentences about missing Wallie, about the fight with the gator, about Gus and the tickets, and killing the gator.

When I paused to find the right word to describe the smell rising from the hell-belly, and the sight of the demon materializing from the foliage, Gus said, "What are you doing?"

"Writing, telling what happened. I won't use your name."

Gus's face was red with either fear or anger. He'd realized the possible consequences of appearing in the feature.

"No one will know it's you, unless you tell them."

I assured Gus that when I published the feature, no one would ever discover he was involved.

The soreness in my hip from the tail's lash, and the stinging in my calf, would not go away for a while. I pulled up my pants leg: a bruise was already beginning to swell, but there was no broken bone.

With the details fresh in mind, I scratched down specifics about carving the pike and confronting the monster. I made notes to calm myself, and threw a few darts, as editors call scoring points of argument or observation. In this case, facts sounded stranger than fantasy, the real more surreal than likely.

As I wrote, my anger cooled, and I recognized the alligator had only acted for survival. In fact, that it had survived at all in such an environment was a kind of miracle. The creature had only followed the course nature prescribed. I didn't feel shame for my actions exactly, but sad regret. We always feel depressed after an outburst of anger.

"Alright, Shakespeare, we have to go," Gus said. He handed me something he'd written on his pad, a third ticket. It was not for arrest, but for cutting the sapling on Park land, and killing wildlife. An appearance in court would not be to his advantage.

I hurried to scrawl a few more sentences.

"Come on," Gus said, "I'll show you that damned waterfall."

At that instant Wallie came trotting out of the trees, dragging a cord some hiker had tied to his collar.

THE WONDERFUL CITY

The most frightening thing about an epidemic was its invisibility. It came in the night, or in bright daylight, and could not be seen or heard or touched as it wreaked its horrors. Before you knew it was present, the affliction raged with high fever, delirium, passing blood, in homes up and down the river valley.

When Billy thought of typhoid, he imagined a giant stepping over hills, breathing venom and swinging a long razor. With every lurch the fiend cut the face or neck of a neighbor and the deadly poison sank in. It was a devil bigger and more wicked than any he'd heard of in stories and gossip. For this specter was blind and wielded the razor when anyone moved or spoke. The killer, who could not see, could not be seen. There was no way to avoid its approach. If you ran, you might crash right into its evil arms.

When rumors of the epidemic began, Billy dreamed each night about the typhoid Satan, taller than the highest mountain, stumbling over ridge and valley,

slaying all in his way. Five years before, there'd been
the awful Spanish flu that took so many lives, including
his Grandma's. That scourge had finally faded when
he was eight or nine. But he recalled the terror, as
grownups watched for symptoms, and the relief when
most of the family were spared. At the age of almost
fourteen he was all too aware of the numbing fear the
word typhoid provoked.

Long before Billy was born, there had been an
outbreak of typhoid in the river valley. About half the
population died of the fever. Billy had seen graves of
victims taken by that horror. Every family in every cove
had mourned as they watched loved ones succumb to
internal bleeding, so the old folks said. The memories
were so painful survivors only whispered of the ordeal,
by fireplaces on windy nights. Crops rotted in fields;
cows went un-milked and unfed. Foxes killed chickens
escaped from henhouses. Springs and wells were
contaminated, and those who drank died of typhoid.
Church meetings were canceled, and there was no
school. Warning signs were posted on gateposts, and
there was no visiting. Roads washed out and were not
repaired. Pigs roved the woods and fields, and rooted
in gardens abandoned to weeds. The only medicine
available was corn liquor, and a few herbs. The liquor
was taken internally, and also rubbed on fevered bodies
to cool them. But whiskey could not stop the intestinal
bleeding. Adults were reluctant to speak to children
about the siege of fever.

Billy had heard Papa say that typhoid was unpredictable.
Two people who lived together, ate the same meals,
drank the same water, slept in the same bed, might have
opposite responses. One could sicken and die, while the
other was untouched, or at worst suffered what was called
"walking typhoid." With walking typhoid, a person might
experience a slight fever, soreness or weakness, and then
recover, as if from a cold. The mystery, the gamble, made
the disease yet more terrifying, for someone who appeared

to have walking typhoid could also sicken suddenly and die within a day or two.

In 1924 the first reports of typhoid came from up the river. That was alarming because it was believed the fever traveled downstream. It was associated with water and water worked its way from springs and runoff to puddles, branches, creeks, and river. If the outbreak started further downstream you were lucky; if upstream you were in danger. This time the first case appeared in the Ward family, near the headwaters, where the river was no more than a creek, and farms just cultivated strips along the banks.

The threat was enough to change everything. Papa ordered Billy and his little sister Annie to stay home, visit no friends. There would be no church, no school, no singing school, no swimming in the river, no fishing, no church picnics, no trips to town or even to the store along the highway. Until the epidemic passed, they would remain at home.

To Billy and Annie it was good news that they wouldn't have to attend school or church. In the summer Preacher Rice's sermons were interminable in the boiling sanctuary. The schoolhouse stank of sweat. If they couldn't swim in the river, they could make wading ponds in the branch, build forts and playhouses under the white pines, climb trees, pick blackberries, when not working in the fields. On rainy days they would play hide-and-seek in the barn loft, on hot days climb the mountain to enjoy a breeze on the summit.

With school closed and church meetings suspended, there was no way for Billy to meet his friend Johnny, who lived on Mount Olivet. Since they were small boys, they'd played kickball together, marbles, made bows and arrows, dammed ponds on the branch, rolled rocks off the mountaintop, stolen apples and grapes from neighbors' yards. But with the quarantine signs on every house, each was trapped, Johnny on Mount Olivet, Billy in the valley.

The epidemic didn't spare Billy from work. There was no end to the jobs Papa found for him: hoeing potatoes, corn, picking beans, carrying firewood for the kitchen stove, cleaning out cow stalls and the horse stall, pulling weeds for the hog. He did more work than ever, now that he was almost fourteen. Each night, exhausted, he stumbled into bed. Grubbing up stumps was the worst, along with digging post holes.

When Billy slipped away on Wednesday morning just after breakfast, to walk to Mount Olivet, he knew Papa would be furious, and handy with his belt. But he would worry about the punishment later, for he had to get away, from work, from the quarantine, and see others, especially his friend. He had to escape, for a day. And when he reached Mount Olivet, with a view over the other mountains and valleys, even to the far towns of Hendersonville and Asheville, he was as thrilled as Johnny was to see him. They stayed away from Johnny's house, for it was quarantined too, and spent much of the day building a tree house beyond the pasture, hammering boards in the forks of a black oak, and sampling plums from a nearby orchard.

Late in the afternoon it was time to descend the mountain and face the worst. The day was still hot, and as he walked Billy was overwhelmed by thirst. There were no springs by the road, and he was parched. He came to a bend in the road where seepage from a cliff rippled along a ditch. The water was mostly clear, with patches of moss around the rocks.

Billy dropped to his knees and drank. The rill tasted of earth and moss, and something else he couldn't name. Then he hurried down the mountain. As he approached the house he steeled himself for what was sure to come. But it had been worth it, just to get away a few hours, to build the treehouse, see his friend. He passed the church locked with a sign on the door, then rounded the bend.

What he saw first was his little sister Annie waiting in the road. She was always a tattler. She ran to the house to tell, and before he reached the yard Mama and Papa and Annie came out, and Mama ran to hug him. "Boy, where have you been?" Papa snarled. Because he had been gone so long, they'd worried he might have fallen into the river, been bitten by a rattlesnake, or run away from home. All were relieved, and Mama wiped away tears; strangely, Papa never mentioned any punishment.

On Thursday and Friday Billy worked harder than ever to make up for his truancy. Papa put him to pulling fodder, the hottest and dirtiest job of the year, stripping lower leaves of corn for horse provender. Sting worms and hornets infested the rows, but he was stung only once, on the neck.

The following Monday, Billy began to feel odd. Sights and sounds didn't quite match, and the ground tilted like the deck of a boat in a storm. His feet grew heavy.

"Why is your face so red?" Mama said, when he came to the house for dinner.

"It's the Dog Days heat," Papa said.

Mama touched his forehead and found he had a fever.

Billy looked at his plate and pushed it away. The table was close, then faraway, voices loud, then distant.

"Did you drink anything on Mount Olivet?" Mama said.

Billy shook his head, then recalled slaking his thirst from the ditch by the road. He decided not to mention that.

Mama wiped his forehead with a wet cloth. That was when the ache in his bones worsened, a throbbing he remembered from the time he had scarlet fever. His bones hurt as if they'd been beaten and bruised.

"He can't go back to the field," Mama said.

"Just a summer cold," Papa said.

Mama helped him to the bedroom and took off his clothes. When he lay back he heard drumming in the air. The light from the window stabbed his eyes. Mama closed the curtains, but his eyes stung, and gave him a headache. The headache spread around his temples, and reached his face.

As he slept, the bed began to move, as if sliding without friction, touching nothing. The walls vanished and he floated over fields and woods, over the river. The bed drifted above hollows and ridges, and above Mount Olivet. He could see Johnny in the treehouse below, and the plum tree in the orchard, and farther out, the highway to a town or city, and further still rose the Black Mountains.

The bed lifted higher yet, and beyond the mountains he saw a city with tall buildings, lofty as skyscrapers he'd noticed in magazines. Glorious parks and wide avenues teemed with buses and automobiles. Children on roller skates swept down the sidewalks. Pigeons veered in clouds over the parks. A large clock on the side of a tower chimed. Beyond the city loomed farther mountains, peaks covered with snow.

I'm dreaming, Billy thought. I have a fever and I'm dreaming. But then the bed began tipping forward, and, as he tried to hold onto the sides, he started to slide. Far below he saw fields, and roads tiny as hairs. There was nothing to grab, and he fell into emptiness, falling, falling, until his head burst, and he knew nothing more.

Billy woke in the morning much cooler. The ache in his limbs hadn't gone away, but felt distant, bearable. Light in the darkened room hurt and he closed his eyes. Insects clicked in the grass outside, crickets and grasshoppers, and cicadas rasped in the trees beyond. He was almost normal.

When Mama entered and saw him awake, she placed a hand on his forehead. "The fever is gone," she said. "Thank the Lord."

Little sister Annie stood in the door watching. Papa appeared and touched his forehead.

"Maybe he just has walking typhoid," Papa said.

"I pray it's so," Mama said. She brought a glass of water

and a warm biscuit with jelly on it. She said anybody with a fever shouldn't drink milk, and must eat only the softest things. When he finished the biscuit she brought another. The jelly looked like melted rubies

Billy would have swung out of bed, but the weakness in his legs and soreness in his bones encouraged him to stay a little longer. All morning he thought about what he'd do when he was better. He'd climb the highest pine on the mountain and look over the valley, seeing what a hawk sees. He'd swim in the river in the hole scooped out at the bend. He'd find the biggest watermelon in the patch and cool it in the spring. He'd ask for his own .22 rifle.

Mama brought him creamed corn and a biscuit for dinner, but by then he didn't feel so cool, or hungry. Little noises echoed inside his head. He threw up, and when Mama pressed his forehead she said the fever had returned. Annie came into the room and asked if Billy was going to die. "Hush up," Mama said.

As he floated into sleep he thought he was climbing the ridge to Mount Olivet. Trees, big oaks, stood in his way, and boulders the size of houses. The ground was so steep he kept slipping back, grabbing trees, clawing dirt. Black flies screamed in his ears. A hornet stung his neck and mosquitoes whined around his eyes.

"Come on, come on," someone called above him.

With immense effort, dodging limbs that raked his cheeks, Billy reached a field on the summit where a breeze soothed his face and swept away mosquitoes. He regained his breath, and saw sparkling in the noonday sun a distant, beautiful city. Windows shone, and roads glistened. Fabulous buildings and parks multiplied beyond counting: bicycles, zoos, automobiles, motorcycles, a Ferris wheel, swimming pools where girls were bathing.

Billy's task was to descend to the incredible valley and make his way to the city bigger than Asheville and Hendersonville combined. A train puffed along tracks to the city. A hundred shops offered white ice cream cones. An airplane took off from a field beyond the city. It was the city of his destiny. All he had to do was take the winding road into the valley, and follow the highway.

When he reached the entrance to the road, cooled by the shade of giant oaks, Billy began to run. He had to reach the city before it vanished, or floated beyond his reach, into the future. As he rounded a bend he saw ahead the biggest dog he'd ever imagined. Its shoulders were high as a Shetland pony's. But it was not size alone that made him stop. Lather hung from the jaws, and it lurched when it stepped forward. The eyes were red.

Billy knew that to show friendliness you held your hand out to a dog to demonstrate no harm was intended. But when he extended his arm to this mammoth canine it didn't seem to notice, though it growled. It was only then he recognized it was mad. The fevered eyes could hardly see; the wide nose couldn't smell. Yet the beast seemed to know he was there, and tilted its ugly head to listen. The cur took a step and stumbled, then advanced at an angle in his direction.

Billy was about to run when the dog fell again and rolled on the ground, then lay still, stretching across the narrow tracks. It seemed to sleep. Could he possibly ease past and continue his journey to the wonderful city? If he tried to go around through the woods, his feet in the leaves would make a disturbing noise. Besides, the woods were tangled with briars and vines, too thick to penetrate.

Billy stepped closer to the monster dog, so close he could smell its hot, fevered, fetid scent, like its flesh was half cooked, its breath the fumes of burned filth. Yet, if he could step around the massive head he might resume his way. With measured, hesitant moves, he was within feet of the slobbering jaws, when the beast growled and rose. The frothy mouth lunged for Billy's leg.

Jumping back as a tooth ripped his pants, Billy fell and rolled away. The mammoth dog faltered then pitched forward. The foaming mouth bit his wrist like a serrated bear trap. It took all Billy's strength to wrestle the arm free, push himself up, and run. When he looked back, the dog was not pursuing. At the edge of the field he stopped to examine his bleeding wrist. The mad-dog's saliva had mixed with his own blood, which meant he was infected with rabies, hydrophobia. There was nothing anybody could do. He would go mad, terrified of water. People would flee him, as lather drooled from his lips.

When Billy woke the next morning he was cool again, but weak, and shaky from the brutal dream. He raised his right wrist, grateful there was no blood or bite marks. He didn't have rabies after all. But as he drew the wrist near his nose, he caught the scent of the rabid dog, the half-cooked smell of flesh burned by fever, half-dead skin, singed by disease. The stink in the dream was his own.

"You're cool again," Mama said when she brought him biscuits and jelly.

Billy's eyes hurt, and he looked away from the door where Anne stood again. "Are you going to heaven?" she asked.

"Would you like grits or oatmeal?" Mama said.

Billy asked for oatmeal with raisins. Mama brought him another biscuit with blackberry jelly. The jelly was so sweet it hurt his taste-buds.

Later, Mama washed his face and chest. If he was a little stronger he'd get out of bed and find the tobacco hidden in the barn and cut off a chew. Tobacco made him feel stronger and more assured. Papa chewed tobacco, but warned Billy not to. The tobacco was his secret pleasure.

That afternoon, as he considered rising from bed, the fever returned. The ache in his bones was the first sign, and the smell of a peculiar smoke, as if his flesh was smoldering. By suppertime the bed was tilting again.

In his sleep Billy dreamed of climbing the mountain to view the glorious city. It was a municipality both clean and luminous, no filth of chicken house nor cow

stall, no smell of hog pen. It was the city described in
the Bible with streets of gold and walls of precious
stones. It was a city with everything he'd ever desired,
or imagined, ponies, girls in white dresses, swimming
pools, streams with giant trout, six-guns, high-powered
rifles. There was a sporting goods store with bows and
arrows, little speedboats with real gasoline motors,
model airplanes with engines. On the walls hung
hunting knives and Swiss Army gadgets.

There were statues in the beautiful city of men on
horses, higher than oak trees, horses so big they could
hide men inside like the Trojan horse in books, horses
made of metal that turned blue. A fountain sprayed
water from a lion's mouth, and there was a pond where
children sailed little boats among geese and swans.

To reach the perfect city he had to follow the road
under the trees. As he hurried he was relieved the mad-
dog was gone. The tracks ran beneath a cliff stuck with
lichens and moss. As he passed under the rock he looked
for rattlesnakes, but saw only a snake skin left like a
warning. A little farther on he heard something move in
a tree ahead, and spotted an animal silhouetted against
the sky, a panther, a long black panther, crouching just
over the road.

Billy knew the most dangerous choice was to run, for
that would trigger the cat's instinct to chase. It would
pursue, leap on his back, and kill. Could he back away
without provoking it? Could he stand still and stare at
it, the way Davy Crocket had stared down a coon ?
Could he keep walking, hoping the cat would not be
aroused by a human acting without apparent fear? The
panther looked ready to pounce.

As he pondered and hesitated, panic overcame him.
Without making a decision, he turned and ran. As he
sprinted, limbs shook behind and the big cat hit the road
with a thud. Pursuing steps accelerated, and he couldn't
look back. Claws sank into his back and shoulders, and
teeth like daggers stabbed into the back of his neck.

Billy heard voices that reminded him the panther was just part of a dream. "Billy, I'm Dr. Lutz, and I'm here to help you. I want you to drink this glass of medicine." His head was lifted and the rim of glass pressed on his lips. He tried to swallow, but much of the liquid ran down the sides of his chin. The warm fluid tasted like tea made from roots and bark. He knew the flavor, but couldn't remember the name.

Billy was so weak he slipped back to sleep and was awakened again as Mama washed his face and arms and chest. "Billy, can you hear me?" she said.

"Just let him sleep," the doctor said.

Billy opened his eyes for an instant, and light seared like beams of fire. He didn't see Anne standing in the doorway.

As he slept again, Billy rose, as though climbing up, up, like Jack and the Beanstalk, past the roof of the house, past treetops, past the mountaintop, lifting past clouds, and the highest hawk. Was he on his way to heaven? outer darkness? When he stopped rising he was at the door of the schoolhouse and Mr. Bishop beckoned him inside. The schoolhouse hovered far above the earth. "I have been waiting for you," the teacher said. He held the blue spelling book. Spelling was Billy's worst subject. Mr. Bishop liked to assign long words with mysterious spelling.

"If you fail you will be pushed off to fall forever," Mr. Bishop said and smiled.

Billy sat at a desk and the teacher called out an impossibly long word. Billy tried to see the word in his mind, but couldn't. He started spelling and stumbled, unable to complete the word.

"Wrong!" Mr. Bishop shouted with glee.

Billy knew he had only three chances. If he misspelled all he was out, which would mean falling from the schoolhouse door forever.

The teacher raised the spelling book like a shield and whispered the second, also a long word with few

vowels, only consonants, a foreign type of word. Billy
sweated as he tried to picture the word, the sequence of
letters. He stammered and stopped.

"Incorrect!" Mr. Bishop laughed.

There was one more chance that he wouldn't be
thrown out of the door higher than the tallest mountain.
Billy's hands were hot and trembling. The spelling book
grew bigger and bigger, its wings wider than an eagle
soaring at him. The fateful book must weigh a hundred
tons. If it dropped on him it would smash him. The
book advanced to drive him toward the door.

The word Mr. Bishop called out was short, but Billy
knew it was a trick word, with weird letters that couldn't
be heard in the pronunciation. Did it begin with "k" as
in knife, or "g" as in gnaw, or gnat. He tried to see the
word, but couldn't.

"You have thirty seconds," Mr. Bishop sang.

The spelling book stretched wide as the room, dark
as a buzzard coming to tear his flesh, peck out his eyes.
The wings blocked all light.

"Time's up." Mr. Bishop giggled.

Billy was thrown backward, by a force he couldn't see,
off the bench, across the floor, dragged to the door and
pushed by the spine of the spelling book into emptiness.
Kicking, he tried to find a foothold on thin air, but fell,
and fell.

When he woke, Billy was not cool as on other morn-
ings. His face was masked in sweat, and he shivered,
remembering the spelling torture and long fall. "You've
got to drink some of this," Mama said. What he felt on
his lips was cool as spring water and smelled of lemon.
Mama had made lemonade. The liquid soothed his dry
tongue and sensitive throat. Though weak, he continued to sip. The lemon taste cleaned his mouth.

When the lemonade was gone, Billy smelled himself.
He gave off an odor of sweat and fever, cooked skin,
partly baked flesh. The smell was not just coming from

his skin but inside, in his breath and sweat. It was the stink of deep disease. When he opened his eyes light flew at him like screaming crows. Again, he didn't see Annie at the door.

Billy hoped that when he dreamed he would not have to spell, but see the wondrous city, and not find his way barred. He would surmount the steep ridge and look over, like Moses sighting the Promised Land. But as he dissolved into sleep he dropped deeper and deeper. He sank under the bed, under the floor, below the cellar, into caves and layers of rock, into tunnels and streams deep in earth. He fell until he was directly under the beautiful city. He must rise through rock and filth to reach the street and parks.

He knew he was dreaming, but the dream was so intense he couldn't stop it. The dream pulled him the way a magnet charms iron. He couldn't escape the dark and the smell of the tunnels under the city. He was underwater and needed to swim upward. It was too dark to see much, but he touched floating things, manure from stables, human waste, offal from butchers' shops, rotten guts, something he thought was a doll but found was a baby still attached to an umbilical cord. A green corpse turned and drifted in a pool tinted with blood. He had to breathe, but couldn't in such carrion-infested water.

Billy struggled to find the surface, but his hands hit more putrefying parts of animals, swollen bodies of dogs, snakes with mouths open, a face with mice in its eyes. He had to breathe, but couldn't. His chest swelled and his throat was about to burst. He would not have guessed such horrors lay beneath the beautiful city. But this was just a dream.

When he finally surfaced from the rotten water there was just enough light to see teeming animals on the shelves of the sewer. Rats the size of cats scurried in all directions among refuse from the city above: decaying vegetables like tomatoes, potatoes, and chicken bones, hog bones, dead cats, pigeon feathers, guts half-eaten. The stench was strangling. Billy looked for a spot where he could climb out of sewage. He couldn't put his hands among the rats. He splashed water on a ledge and rats spread aside.

It took all his strength to pull himself out of the ooze. A rat nipped his left hand and fled. He slapped at other rodents, and slipped back into the fetid lagoon. Straining harder, he hoisted himself to the ledge and kicked and slapped at rats to scatter them. Billy crawled on elbows and knees to a place where he could stand.

Stepping around the rodents, Billy stumbled along the ledge until he saw a circle of light overhead. Closer, he saw the illuminated ring was daylight around the rim of something. Pushing, he found the object was metal, and heavy. Shoving harder, he saw the thing was a large coin, like a medallion, eighteen inches across. He lifted the thick lid, which rang as it rolled aside.

Sunlight, so intense it shocked him, shot into the pit. He shielded his eyes until they adapted a little to the apocalyptic brightness, then heaved himself into open air.

After Billy blinked, and turned his face away, he could hardly take in the sight around him. Buildings white and pink with walls of glass soared into the sky in early light. Sidewalks moved like conveyor belts in both directions, and people soared above the streets on little platforms, holding to handlebars. Wide buildings had gardens on ledges. There were no electric or telephone lines. Billy expected streets paved with gold, as described in the Bible, but instead the pavements were transparent as glass or ice.

He stepped onto a moving sidewalk which carried him to a park, where he jumped off. A drinking fountain offered Coca-Cola instead of plain water. He gulped as much as he could hold. Boys sailed boats on a pond among swans. Girls sunbathed in the grass wearing nothing. He turned away, then looked again.

Stores lined the street around the park. The one he'd dreamed about before displayed sports equipment in its window, baseballs, and baseball gloves and uniforms, bats of every size, shoes with spikes, leggings red and blue. There were also fishing rods of different kinds and lengths, and large revolvers of magnum caliber.

"What would you like?" a clerk at the entrance said. Before Billy could answer the man handed him a flyrod, the finest he'd ever seen. The tip of the rod twitched as he walked back to the park where a band was playing.

A voice said, "I wish the fever would come down. If it rises more you should rub him in alcohol."

He wanted to return to the dream, to the fishing rod, to the band playing, and the girls lying in the sun, and people flying on little platforms. But the city faded beyond recovery, the fabulous city which he'd entered with such difficulty. Instead, he smelled his broiled skin, the scent of old flesh. The voices were faraway.

When Billy woke again he was lifted off the sheet and rubbed with an icy cloth over his face and arms, his chest and back. Even his legs were washed with chilling liquid. They scrubbed every part of his body, then started again. The burned smell of his skin was wiped away. He shivered and shuddered as they wrapped him in sheets again.

"High fever can affect the brain," a voice said. Water was poured over his hair, and ran into his ears.

"The next twenty-four hours will tell," the voice said.

Billy thought he heard someone praying. It was Papa's voice. He listened for Annie's voice, but couldn't distinguish it.

As Billy faded into sleep again he knew he would dream of the wonderful city. Even so, he was surprised to find himself walking a long and winding road that ascended hills and dropped into ravines. From the hilltops he could view the city gleaming in the distance, the buildings even higher than he remembered, of glass and marble. Towers multiplied and answered the sunlight. Domes loomed like large heads. Faraway he could discern people soaring and circling on flying platforms, like butterflies among roses.

Climbing hills, Billy grew tired and thirsty. Water ran in ditches along the road, but he dared not drink. Weak from typhoid, he shouldn't be out walking. But he had to return to the city. Only the wonderful city could make him well, heal the infection inside him. Besides, he had walking typhoid: he had typhoid, and he was walking. He laughed at the joke.

As he drew closer, he saw the wall of the city, and outside the wall, a park, which appeared to be a miniature replica of the city itself. But, looking closer, he saw what he'd taken for model buildings were tombstones, monuments like little skyscrapers. Stone houses the size of chicken coops covered the graves. Stone angels watched over the dead, and columns and statues rose above all. Then he saw fresh dirt piled beside a rectangular hole, and a procession followed a coffin carried by six men. They lowered the box into the ground and heaped flowers on the grave. Even in the wonderful city there was death.

Sweat like burning dew formed on his forehead and ran into his eyes. He wiped the moisture away to see clearly the splendid metropolis. If he didn't keep it in view the glorious vision might disappear. Only his sight could preserve the marvel intact. He concentrated on the vista of minarets and spires that touched the clouds. The panorama drew him as a pilgrim is led to a shrine.

Thirst burned in his throat, and his lips and tongue were swollen with dryness. He had to find a drink and he had to reach the blessed city looming nearer and higher. The road crossed a bridge, but the stream below it was polluted with dead birds, poison with decay. A sign said "Do Not Drink." The road was dusty, and dust loaded weeds and leaves along the way.

His mouth was so dry Billie feared it might shatter like glass. The city appeared to retreat as he approached. He would walk faster if he had the strength. Only after he labored over a final hill did he see how high the wall rose around the city. The wall was a fortress of white and pink marble, higher than an oak tree, wider than a house. There was a door, but the door was fast. Many people gathered along the top of the wall. Behind the wall, buildings bright as mirrors leapt into the sky. Windows in the wall watched him.

As he stumbled closer, Billy noticed a table at the foundation of the wall, an ordinary table about ten feet long. Three people sat behind the table, a woman, a man, and a child. Two vessels sat on the table before them. As he approached, the woman, who wore a white cloth over her hair, proclaimed in a stern voice, "To enter the city you must pass a test."

"What kind of test?" Billy answered.

"A simple test," the man said. The man and the child wore cloths over their heads also, like figures from Bible pictures. Only then did Billy recognize the man as Mr. Bishop, the spelling teacher, and the child was his sister Annie.

"What are you doing here?" he asked Annie.

"She cannot answer," the woman declared.

With the white cloths over their heads, the three resembled figures in a Christmas pageant.

One vessel on the table was a large crystal goblet filled with clear water. The other was a small bowl around which gnats swarmed.

"We know you're thirsty," the woman said. "You can drink from only one vessel. If you choose the wrong one you may not enter the city."

Billy studied the large goblet brimming with cool water. The glass sparkled with rainbows and flashes of sunlight. A water-strider rested on the surface of the bowl, and gnats lit on the rim.

"To enter you must sate your thirst from the correct one," the woman warned. Billy examined the face of the spelling teacher, and Annie's expression. Neither offered him any clue. From the woman's hard look he knew what he was required to do: it was a trick. To enter the glorious city, he had to drink from the dirty bowl. It was obvious she expected him to choose the elegant cup filled with clean water.

Billy grabbed the warm bowl, and as he gulped he saw a worm in the liquid. He closed his eyes and swilled all the container held, and set the bowl down. When he looked up he saw thousands on the wall watching.

"You are forbidden to enter the hallowed city," the woman announced. She turned her back, as did the man and Annie. Those on the wall turned away also.

This is only a dream, Billy prayed, only a dream.

There was no choice but to retreat from the shining city. To keep the immaculate towers in view he walked backwards, as though withdrawing from royalty, reluctant to accept the failure of his quest. People soared around the temples and skyscrapers, free as eagles or angels. He kept his eyes on the radiant splendors until he dropped behind the first hill, then turned and began trudging toward the familiar mountains.

When Billy woke, Mama was washing his face with a cool cloth. She was dressed in her best clothes. Papa stood by, in his Sunday suit.

"Are you going to church?" Billy said.

"We'll be gone for about an hour."

Billy realized how cool he was, weak but calm. The light in the bedroom was ordinary.

"You rest and we'll be back soon. The fever broke last night."

Billy was thirsty and hungry, empty as a shrinking balloon.

Mama set a tray beside the bed, holding a glass of water and a plate of biscuits with blackberry jelly.

"We'll be back in an hour," Mama said, and then they were gone.

Billy gulped the water and grabbed a jelly biscuit. The warm bread tasted too good to describe. He ate with renewed relish, and tried to recall more about the radiant city, and the tribunal that denied him entry, which included little sister Annie. Only then did it occur to him he hadn't seen Annie with Mama and Papa when they left for church, and he recalled the fresh-dug grave outside the luminous city.

DEVIL'S COURTHOUSE

In theory gold can be found almost anywhere. It can even be extracted from sea water, though the cost is prohibitive. But more often gold is found in veins or lodes with quartz, or mixed with silver ore, or washed out of the bellies of mountains into streams where it can be panned. As a professor of archeology at a small college in central North Carolina, I knew that gold was most commonly found in the Old North State in the Piedmont, in the counties sometimes called the Gold Belt: Cabarrus, Davidson, Guilford, McDowell, Randolph. North Carolina had been the largest supplier of gold for the United States Mint, until the discovery of nuggets at Sutter's Mill in California, January, 1848. None of the productive gold mines in the state was located in the western mountain region.

You might guess my surprise when it was reported that a nugget almost the size of a tennis ball had been found by a hunter in the high mountains of Pisgah National Forest west of Asheville. The hunter told reporters he'd made the find in the woods below Devil's Courthouse, near the crest of the Blue Ridge Mountains and the scenic highway called the Blue Ridge Parkway. Devil's Courthouse is a cliff that rears up from the balsam forest like the tower of a fortress, and soars into the sky with a few wind-stunted trees clinging to its top. It's a sight well known to tourists on the Parkway.

Everyone should be excited by the discovery of gold, especially at such an unlikely place and elevation. And where there's one nugget there may be many more. But what was discovered near the nugget also caught my attention. Soon after noticing the nugget in the leaves the hunter found some bones, and, looking further, uncovered a human skeleton. State forensic experts, examining the skeleton, declared the remains to be Native American. And with the bones a piece of rusting chain and an iron shackle were discovered. The combination of the nugget, bones, and manacle or fetter was significant. As a student of the Cherokees I knew I had to investigate.

Throughout history, the discovery of gold nuggets has precipitated a rush. In North Carolina in 1803, in north Georgia in the 1820s, in California in 1848-49, and in the Klondike in 1898, news of a gold strike brought hordes of frantic prospectors to claim, dig, fight, kill, and spoil the land. I was certain that news of the find below Devil's Courthouse would bring thousands of gold seekers, tearing into the woods with picks and shovels, guns, axes, chainsaws, GPS. People searching for gold are no longer law-abiding, or even rational. The stories of gold madness in California, South Dakota, and the Yukon, are well known, the stuff of legend, fiction, and Hollywood. I was sure masses would be climbing the mountain beyond Looking Glass Rock or descending from the Parkway to find the lode from which the giant nugget came. There would be a frenzy to locate the source. Digging was not permitted in the National Forest, but that would not stop those who imagined a fortune waited to be claimed high on the government land. I loaded my station wagon with a few tools and supplies and camping equipment and started out the next morning, telling my wife I'd be back in time to teach my classes on Monday afternoon.

It always thrilled me to drive west from the Piedmont into the mountains. From a distance the blue chain of ridges suggests a cleaner, cooler, higher world. For me it was like driving back in time. I grew up on a farm in those mountains, a hardscrabble farm, a one-horse farm I'd been happy to escape to attend college. But whenever I return I still get that stiffening in the back of my throat when I see Mt. Mitchell in the distance, as the Interstate sweeps above the hollows and remote coves, soaring over little farms like the one I grew up on.

As a teenager I'd hunted deer with my dad in Pisgah National Forest, so I knew something about the terrain below Devil's Courthouse. Most of that range is covered with hardwoods, beech, oak, hickory, maple. At one time the woods were dominated by giant chestnut trees, but those died in the blight of 1924. When I was a boy the white skeletons of the chestnuts still loomed over living trees on the mountainsides. But those goliaths had long since fallen and rotted at the feet of the lesser survivors. At elevations of more than five thousand feet the hardwoods give way to spruce and fir trees, called "balsams" by the local people. In the Ice Age the spruce and firs covered all the ridges, but with warming of the hemisphere the conifers retreated to higher peaks in the chain. "Islands of Canada," the summits are sometimes called.

Though their villages were mostly located farther west and south, on the tributaries of the Tennessee River, the mountains always seemed to me haunted by the Cherokees. As a boy hoeing corn, I turned up arrowheads and pieces of pottery in the loam along the creek. My dad said if you listened to the murmur of the river or the roar of a waterfall, you could hear the Indians talking or singing. He said that even the wind in the mountains still spoke Cherokee, and the soil contained the bodies of Indians far older than the Cherokees. That was one reason I became an archeologist, to study the native cultures of the mountain region, primarily Cherokee, but also Catawba, Chickamauga, and even Muskogee, and other Woodland tribes who had preceded them.

Imagine my surprise when I approached the parking area on the Parkway below Devil's Courthouse and saw only half a dozen cars and a park ranger's SUV. I'd expected to find multitudes, and vehicles overflowing the parking area and lining the highway, people wild to dig up the mountain to find gold. Instead, I noticed a young couple standing at the look-out, and rather than studying the giant cliff that rose far above, they focused on the smart phones in their hands. An older couple sat at one of the picnic tables, but they were studying their iPads also. A group of three young men were walking up the path toward the top of the cliff, but each was talking on a cell phone.

It seemed no one but me had noticed the article about the large gold nugget and the skeleton. Was I the only one left who read newspapers? Had I dreamed the discovery of the nugget and Indian bones? Had the gold-seekers already come and gone? The park ranger sat in the SUV and I walked over to the driver's window.

"Where's the crowd?" I said.

"Probably at the Asheville Mall," he said with a shrug.

"I expected hoards looking for gold."

"So did we, but no one seems to have noticed." The ranger added that young people now don't even bother to hunt. The forest was overrun by deer, since only the elderly hunted anymore. "The young are afraid of the woods," he said.

I showed him my ID and told him I was certified by the state to examine Native sites.

"Just don't do any digging," the ranger said. "And if

you see anyone digging let us know. Federal law forbids disturbing Native remains."

"Yes, I do know," I said, putting a little reserve in my voice.

The ranger looked me in the eye. "If you see a man with a long beard let us know," he said.

"A hunter?"

"No, escapee from the mental wing of the VA hospital near Asheville. A deranged Vietnam vet. It's rumored he's somewhere in the forest."

I was as relieved as the ranger that the crowds hadn't converged on Devil's Courthouse to delve for nuggets, but disappointed too, to think people were so preoccupied with themselves they wouldn't bother to look for gold, or an unusual Native site. If there had been smart phones in 1849 there might not have been a Gold Rush. I assured the ranger I only wanted to examine the site at this point. Maybe later I would seek permission to dig.

The ranger got out of the vehicle and walked to the overlook to point out the spot below the base of the cliff where the nugget and remains had been found. "There's no trail," he said, "so you'll have to bushwhack." His use of the word "bushwhack" told me he was from up North. To bushwhack means to ambush in the Southern highlands.

The mountainside below the Parkway was so steep I walked farther out the ridge to find a gentler slope for my descent. The spruce trees were so thick I had to stoop and wrestle through them, lashed in the face by spiny limbs. Soon as I reached the lower hardwoods I had to hold to trunks to keep from falling, dropping from tree to sapling, holding onto roots and rocks. It took about an hour to work my way down to the area the ranger had pointed to. My feet tore into the leaf pack, stirring up tobacco-like and musty odors.

As I neared the site below the cliff base, I saw where leaves had been disturbed and the ground trampled.

There were several tracks on exposed ground. The team that carried out the skeleton had been there. I saw a cigarette butt and an empty can of a high-energy drink. Dozens had left tracks, a few probably searching for more gold nuggets, others curious about the skeleton and the iron shackle.

I was looking particularly for quartz, because gold is often found in or near quartz. Where the leaves had been disturbed I did find pieces of granite. The base of the cliff was a few hundred yards above me. I climbed in that direction and finally spotted some pieces of white quartz, and then more, chips and flakes, fragments, some shaped almost like arrowheads. I raked away leaves and saw hundreds of pieces of white stone, and broken arrowheads. There was a kind of shelf on the slope that must have served as a workshop for some indigenous craftsman. But because there were only fragments, I couldn't tell if this was a Cherokee site, or had been left by some earlier inhabitants of the mountains, one of the Woodland tribes whose names are lost forever.

Picking through the half-finished and fractured pieces, I found no sign of gold, no glittering specks, nothing that resembled ore. Wherever the hunter had found the large nugget, it did not seem to have come from this ancient weapons factory. I was on my knees examining a larger piece of quartz when I realized someone was standing among the laurel bushes ahead of me. I raised my eyes and saw a tall man in dirty jeans and a red flannel shirt. He had a long beard and wore a wrecked felt hat. He looked like a character from a Hatfield-McCoy film.

"Howdy," I said in my best down-home voice. He didn't answer. I stood up and told him I was studying the place where the Indian skeleton was found.

"Wouldn't linger here if I was you," he said.

"Why not? This is National Forest, public land."

"There's a panther using up here," he said. "There's more skeletons in these woods than the one they found."

Long as I could remember there'd been stories of

panthers lurking in the mountains. Local folks liked to thrill tourists with such tales. In the old days I would have guessed this fellow was a moonshiner with a still nearby. I was an intruder who might stumble on his operation. Most moonshiners had long ago become marijuana growers, but maybe he was a hold-out.

"Have you seen a panther?" I said.

"Many a time."

"And was it a big black cat?" I said with a chuckle. Natives always claimed the panthers they spotted were both big and black.

"Mister, don't say I didn't warn you."

"But you don't seem afraid to linger here yourself."

The man carried in his belt the biggest pistol I'd ever seen, a .44 magnum with a long barrel. "Panthers know I'm ready for them," he said.

"Do you have a permit to carry that on government land?" I said. "You're not allowed to hunt with a hand-gun."

"What permission do you have?" he snapped. I took out my wallet and showed him the permit issued by the State of North Carolina for archeological work on state land. The sight of the official paper seemed to affect him noticeably.

"Don't say I didn't warn you, buddy," he muttered and stepped back, turned and walked into the rhodo-dendrons. It puzzled me that he would risk showing himself if he was a moonshiner. This was too far above water for a moonshine still anyway. Was he a prospector looking for gold nuggets? Could he be the escap-ee from the mental ward in the VA hospital? Could he have a patch of ginseng or marijuana growing some-where on the mountainside?

No explanation I could think of seemed to fit the bearded man's appearance and behavior. From the condition of his clothes and hair and beard he must have been living in the woods a long time. I could imagine him a fugitive from the law, an escapee from prison, but not the disturbed soldier from the Asheville hospital. There was something touching about him warning me, an old mountain boy myself, about a lurking panther. I had no interest in turning him in, whoever he was. Like as not he was now watching me from the thicket.

Everyone knows that gold moves downstream and downhill. If you find a nugget it makes sense to explore higher up to find its source, the vein, the mother lode. I had no equipment for digging, and I didn't plan to dig. I'd just poke around and see what signs turned up. Climbing the slope, I looked for my bearded friend. I didn't relish being surprised again. But no one appeared. Either he was keeping me in his sights from cover, or he'd hightailed it away. Likely he'd done the latter, for logic suggested he needed to put as much distance between himself and me as possible. With luck I wouldn't see him again.

What I did find were more quartz rocks, white quartz, milk quartz we used to call it. Pieces the size of footballs were scattered among the bushes and leaves. They looked like they might have rolled from farther up the slope. I glanced around with every step, but saw only a squirrel running out a limb. Yet it felt as though someone watched me, if not the bearded old-timer then someone else. I climbed another hundred yards and saw a wall of rock ahead. Pushing more bushes aside I found the base of the mighty cliff.

Looking up, I could see the face of Devil's Courthouse looming a thousand feet above. Just staring at the many layers of rock made me feel I was falling backward. I stood at the foundation of something almost too massive and towering to take in. The rock was a residue of the creation of the planet, the once molten matter of the stars.

There was a kind of trail along the bottom of the cliff, and following the trail I came to an overhang with a hollowed-out space beneath it, a sheltered place of the kind my dad called a "hog rock." In the old days when people let their hogs range in the woods until killing time, the swine found places to shelter in beneath cliffs, out of sun in summer, and out of wind and rain, and snow in winter. And from those high vantage points the hogs could monitor slopes below, on the lookout for wolves or bears, or maybe panthers, and even people. And like the hogs, hunters had found these sites perfect for deer stands, protected from the elements, and with wide, commanding views of the woods below. The litter in the dirt under the overhang showed the place had indeed been used by hunters. Empty cartridge casings, sandwich wrappers, lay in the dirt. Maybe the bearded man had hidden here also. But to spend the nights at this elevation he would need more shelter, a cave that reached farther back under a cliff.

I followed the track around the base and found boulders and pieces of granite fallen off the rock face. Some had rolled farther down the slope, and some rested against trees. The boulders were the natural products of time and erosion, freezing and thawing, and wind working on the cliff above. I could have been at the foot of an ancient castle or cathedral. In fact, the cliff above looked like a mammoth work of masonry.

A hundred yards out the trail I came to a cave entrance, partly hidden by laurel bushes. The ground at the opening was worn and packed, like there had been a good deal of traffic in and out. The entrance was tall enough for me to stand in, but I could see little inside. I thought I spotted a pot or can, and maybe a blanket. Was this where the bearded man holed up? Without a flashlight it would be useless to try to look inside. There was a flashlight in my car, but it would take an hour to climb back to the parking area. The afternoon was more than half over.

It was possible that a bear could be denned up in the cave, or indeed a panther sleeping off its nightly hunt. I laughed at the thought, and the bearded man's warning. These caves in the high mountains had served as hide-outs for outliers, the outlaws called bushwhackers during the Civil War, deserters from both armies who preyed on farmers and families in the villages below while the menfolk were away. Rumor was that some of the loot they'd stolen was still hidden in the caves, unclaimed after the outliers were arrested, shot, or vanished. I never knew if there was any truth to those rumors. If the treasures had been found, the finders never told anyone.

Since the afternoon was already far gone, I'd have to wait until tomorrow to return with a flashlight and extra batteries and explore the cave. Reluctantly I turned back to retrace my steps.

That night I stayed in a motel in Brevard, near the entrance to the National Forest. I ate at a nearby restaurant and returned to my room, hoping to watch a movie on the TV. There were more than two hundred channels available, but none offered anything I cared to watch. Even the stuff on the sci-fi channel seemed intended for children. I couldn't get out of my mind the voice of the bearded man who'd warned me off the mountain, then disappeared into the rhododendron thicket. "I wouldn't linger here if I was you," he'd said. "There's a panther using up here. There's more skeletons in these woods than the one they found."

When I was a boy, who loved to roam the woods and fish in summer and hunt squirrels in the fall, I had from time to time encountered moonshiners who warned me away from the area where their stills were located. Usually they carried guns and claimed to be hunting themselves, or looking for bee trees, or ginseng, or sometimes searching for a lost dog. The rifle in the crook of their arm was persuasive, and I always heeded their warnings and turned back.

But there was something different about the bearded man with the .44 magnum pistol. It was unlikely he'd be making liquor or growing marijuana at the high elevation, near the Parkway, at this time of year. He must be a fugitive from prison, or possibly the patient escaped from the ward at the VA hospital, as unlikely as that seemed. It was odd he'd shown himself and warned me away. He could just as well have remained hidden in the thousands of acres of the forest.

That night I dreamed about searching in the woods for gold and old bones. The bearded man appeared in the dream. Instead of a pistol he carried a hypodermic needle, which he threatened to throw at me like a dart, the kind of dart used to tranquilize wild animals. He said I'd invaded his woods and needed to be taught a lesson. I started running away from him, and just as I came to the edge of a cliff and jumped, I woke.

The next morning I stopped at a convenience store to buy an extra flashlight and more batteries. I grabbed a couple of sandwiches and a bag of potato chips, in case I'd be in the woods all day. My dream about the bearded man bothered me. It was just a dream, but there was something disturbing about the memory of him, at the site where the nugget and the Native skeleton had been found. Dreams can be discounted, but I'd seen the man close enough to smell his unwashed clothes and skin, and see the revolver he sported.

The Parkway ranger was at the parking lot below Devil's Courthouse again when I arrived. When he saw the bag of supplies I carried he said, "Please, leave no litter in the woods." I promised him I'd bury any trash brought into the Forest, and I decided not to tell him about the bearded man in the rhododendron thicket.

As the ranger began to make a call on his radio, I started out the trail along the ridge. Took me an hour to reach the base of the cliff and find the cave entrance. There was no sign of the bearded man, and the blanket I thought I'd seen on the cave floor was gone. Had I scared him away? Had he fled, knowing his lair was discovered? If he was insane there could be no predicting what he might do. I stood still and listened, but the only sounds were squirrels in the oaks, a bird I didn't recognize, and traffic on the Parkway above.

As I entered the cave, stabbing the wall of darkness with the flashlight, I was struck by the smell. It was the odor of an old house or barn long abandoned, the scent of mold, mildew, dust, of rotted leather, ashes. The floor was littered with charred logs, rags, rusting tools, various pieces of harness, brown newspapers, even rotted books. There were many bottles and jars, mostly broken. The cave had served as the hideout for many over the years dating back before Confederate times. And there were bones in the dust also, as though deer and bear and smaller animals had been killed and eaten, or come here to die when wounded. Bootleggers, hunters, fugitives, deserters, had found sanctuary there. There were even pieces of broken and rotted furniture, the remains of cots, the rusted barrel of a shotgun.

It was likely the cave had been used by the first hunters and explorers, men like Daniel Boone, and by the Indians long before that. There would be no gold among the flotsam and jetsam. Any nuggets would have been spotted long ago. Prehistoric animals had probably hibernated there, the giant sloth, the saber-toothed cat. I poked into the corners of the cave and prodded the dirt floor, but found nothing to explain the gold nugget and skeleton and shackle found in the woods down the slope.

I was ready to give up and return to the station wagon, but on a whim decided to explore further along the base of the giant cliff. I was no closer to solving the mystery of the bones and the source of the nugget than before, but while there I might as well look around a little, after coming a long way. I almost hoped to see the bearded man again. In retrospect he seemed more hallucination than a real person.

I picked my way through briars and vines for half a mile around the foot of the cliff. The cover was so thick I had to drop into the woods below to find my way. I stopped to listen and felt just a breath of breeze. But the whisper wasn't coming from the trees, and it was a warm breath, in the chill mountain air. The whiff seemed to be issuing from the base of the cliff. And then I noticed leaves and vines near the rock were trembling. Stepping closer I could feel the warm breath on my face, and smell the heated air. In the chilly autumn it was like vapor coming from a furnace deep in the mountain.

Now I knew that large, deep caves often exhale, as warm air from in the earth rises into cooler air outside. And at other times caves seem to inhale. I could definitely feel warmer air coming through the vines and briar stalks, but I couldn't see the source of the current. I wished I had hedge trimmers or a mowing blade to cut away the matted vegetation. As it was, I had only my pocket knife to slash some of the canes. With hands and feet, I pushed away vines, looking for snakes, maybe hornet nests. My hands and wrists got scratched. I hoped there was no poison oak among the tangles of briars. The jungle growth suggested the ground there had once been cleared, possibly by a wildfire.

Rocks had been piled up at the cliff base. Closer to the cliff, I saw no opening, only more rocks. Stones, some big as boulders, were heaped against the wall. But I could hear the whisper of air coming between the rocks, or around the rocks. Air issuing from the cracks was warm and damp, heated by geothermal energy. It carried the scent of earth and rock, and places where rubies might be hidden in deep strata. But mixed with the scent was something else too, which I couldn't identify.

Where exactly was the air coming from? All I could see were heaped rocks and boulders. There was no visible opening in the base of the cliff. Were the stones piled there to conceal an entrance, hidden under briars and vines? I put my hand between two rocks and felt the breath of damp air. Looking around to make sure no one was watching, I began lifting the rocks I could manage away from the heap and letting them roll downhill until they lodged on trees or brush. The boulders were much too big to lift. I couldn't even roll them.

I paused and studied the large rocks. What was needed was a pry-pole, something to give leverage. With my knife I trimmed a thick limb of a fallen oak tree. (No trees could be cut in the National Forest.) Jabbing the pole into the dirt under the biggest boulder I moved it a few degrees, then a little more. Sweating and out of breath, I strained until the rock shifted and rolled down the slope and lodged against a beech. Then I attacked the others.

What I found behind the boulders was a cave mouth about four feet high, stuffed with smaller stones. As I tore away the blockage, the warm airflow grew stronger. I cleared away enough rocks to search the opening, then switched on a flashlight and peered in.

A kind of tunnel entered the mountain, maybe four feet high. I stooped inside and the tunnel opened into a room where I could stand. I played the beam around the walls and ceiling which seemed covered with white mold or powder. And then I heard a buzz that sounded like a baby shaking its rattle. Pointing the light at the floor ahead I saw a large timber rattler, coiled and shaking its tail in a blur. Its head, pointed like an arrow, was aimed at me.

I didn't have a hoe or stick, or axe or gun. Probably the snake had retreated to the cave to sleep through the winter, and I'd awakened it. I swept the light over the floor searching for a rock to throw at the viper. That was when I saw the crude steps cut into the floor of the cave, going down out of sight. Who could possibly have carved steps down into the mountain? It was not likely Cherokees had done such work with their stone tools. There were animal bones in the dust around the steps, but at a distance I couldn't identify them. I needed a closer look, but would have to get past the rattlesnake.

The buzz in the darkness stopped, and when I swung the light back in that direction I saw the snake had uncoiled and was crawling to the left, away from the steps. I waited, following the undulating form with the light until it soaked into a crevice. There were cobwebs all around, quivering in the breeze, and spiders glistened. I hoped none were black widows or brown recluses. A bite could make me too weak to walk back to the car, and I wasn't sure my cell phone would work at that elevation.

The dusty steps were rudimentary and steep and appeared to twist down into the mountain. Among the bones there were rusting tools, things like pick-axes, handles long rotted away. Probably these were the instruments used to carve the steps. There was also gravel and pieces of rock on the steps. Swinging the light from side to side, I descended the first few steps, and peered into the depths. Brushing spider webs aside, I stared into the warm wind. The smell was stronger now than it had been at the entrance, the odor of something ancient and long decayed.

Stepping carefully to avoid falling on stones or bones, I continued down the twisting stairs, and saw chisel marks on the walls. Someone had carved the stairwell with great labor. Could the Cherokees have done such work after acquiring metal tools? Or had some earlier tribe cut the steps into the guts of the mountain? And where did the steps go? It was well known that the Spanish had searched for silver and gold in the mountains after De Soto encountered the Cherokees around 1540. Could the Spanish have carved into the granite below Devil's Courthouse such a flight of steps? A Captain Juan Pardo had led a band of soldiers back into the mountains in 1567, but had not reported finding gold. One of his men had recorded seeing "mines of crystal." There was a rumor that another group of Spanish soldiers had disappeared in the mountains and never been heard from again, but I couldn't remember the date for that expedition.

Farther down I found a piece of timber fallen on the steps, the size of a railroad tie that had been hewn with an axe. I pushed the beam aside and stepped lower. The

breeze got even warmer. I thought of stories I'd heard
as a child from the pulpit about fire and brimstone,
of hell deep under the earth. It was easy to see why
our ancestors believed the Devil dwelt far down in
the ground, tormented by sulfurous fumes and black
flames. Where else could hell be but deep in the earth?
And here I was beneath Devil's Courthouse.

As I descended, the air grew closer and seemed
to have less oxygen. I wondered if it was possible to
suffocate, getting farther from the cave entrance and
open air. Had I ever heard of spelunkers asphyxiated
from bad air in caves? Could fumes of natural gas in
the earth overwhelm you? The danger would be that
you might black out before knowing you were at risk.
If I got short of breath I'd climb back out as quick as I
could. I'd watch myself for any sign of smothering.

When I'd gone down about two hundred feet the
flashlight picked up something white ahead. It was round
and smooth as a volley ball, bigger than a soft ball. I
eased down onto a dirty floor and saw the white object
had two holes in it. It was a skull! And in the dust there
were ribs and arm bones, a whole skeleton. I held the
light closer and saw a rusted iron band on one of the leg
bones. A mostly rusted chain ran out through the dust
and was attached to a ring in the rock wall, and several
other chains were fastened to the ring as well.

Following the other chains with the flashlight, I saw
each led to another skeleton and skull, seven skulls in all.
One chain was broken and not attached to any bones.
Rusting tools lay in the dust with the bones. Maybe
it was the bad air, or the horror of what I'd stumbled
on, but I felt dizzy. Leaning on the cave wall I tried to
imagine what I'd found. It was known the Spaniards had
forced the Indians to dig for gold and silver. Had they left
the Indians here to starve and die, when they abandoned
the mine and returned to Mexico or Spain? The broken
chain must have held the Indian who'd somehow freed
himself but died on the slope below, leaving his skeleton

to be found by the hunter. He'd crawled up the steps carrying a large nugget, and had died maybe of snakebite or a heart attack, or been killed by his captors. The nugget had been hidden on him.

The scene around me in the glittering chamber made me shudder. The sockets in the skulls stared. I knew I should look for gold in the seams of the rock. There was certainly quartz there, gleaming like dew or chandeliers. They must have found gold since the man who made it outside was carrying the nugget. The warm air in the cave was stifling, and I couldn't stop trembling. Hot air from deep in the mountain smelled poisonous.

But then I saw a cross sparkling on the ribs of one of the skeletons, and the remains of a beard fallen away from the jawbone. Cherokees plucked out their beards, and it was unlikely Natives would carry crosses around their necks. I rubbed away dust from the other skeletons and saw more crucifixes on chains and the remains of beards. There was even a signet ring in the dust. Slowly it came to me that these were not Cherokees, but Spaniards who'd died in chains deep in the mine. Had the Cherokees somehow overcome their captors and put them in chains and left them to die? That explained why the mine had been abandoned: the Indians had little use for gold. And the Cherokees had never told anyone what they'd done. The band of Spaniards had simply disappeared from history.

The skeleton found outside was almost certainly not an Indian's but that of a Spaniard who had escaped, carrying the big nugget. The forensic experts had somehow mis-identified the find, seeing only what they expected to find. Maybe they'd not even performed DNA tests on the remains. My astonishment at the discovery made me shorter of breath. I had to get outside, to fresh air.

As I turned back to the steps to make my escape, the flashlight slipped from my hand and rolled away. There was nothing but ultimate darkness. The hot air blowing on my face seemed the wind of madness. I lost all sense of direction, and couldn't really tell up from down They say people caught in a heavy snow storm are in a white-out. I was in a black-out. I took a step in the direction I thought was the stairs, but my foot crunched on a bone. Only then did I remember the other flashlight bought that morning.

What a relief when the spare light worked and I found the steps! Weak from lack of oxygen, I stumbled to the bottom step and began climbing, holding to the wall with my right hand. Coughing, with dust in my throat, I knew I'd be lucky to make it to the upper level, much less to open air. But if I hurried that would use up even more oxygen; better to go slow to keep from passing out.

As I labored on the steps, trying to control my panic, I wondered what I should do about the horror I'd found. Must the authorities be informed of the scene in the gold mine? The Spanish had been punished by those they enslaved. Who should be apprised of the shocking scene deep in the mountain for almost five hundred years? The federal government? The state government? The Cherokee nation? The academic community? Did the public have a right to be informed? Should I write an article about what I'd found? Many would rush to see the skeletons chained in the pit, and maybe to look for gold.

Or should the remains be left in peace where they'd been sealed up for almost half a millennium, undisturbed by tourists, journalists, officials, historians? Did I have an obligation as a scholar to reveal what I'd stumbled on? It could be argued that my discovery was a significant find in the history of the exploitation and colonization of North America. Withholding this information could be viewed as unethical and unprofessional, if not illegal. And even if I didn't reveal what I'd seen, it was possible someone else in the future would find the mine deep in the mountain and publicize it. Discovery was likely, though the date was not certain.

Approaching the top of the steps, I raised the light, hoping not to see my rattlesnake friend. But two eyes reflected the flashlight, two shining beads an inch and a quarter apart. It was a snake, probably the one seen before. I stopped with my face about level with the rattler. Questions about what to do about my discovery suddenly seemed irrelevant, compared to my immediate danger. I had to get out to the open air and the rattlesnake was blocking my way. I needed to reach the daylight before the batteries in the flashlight died. I stood in the sickening breeze pondering my choices.

The snake raised its tail and began the hateful song. It was the sound of a Mexican maraca teasing me, the thresh of dry seeds in a pod. The snake sounded like a jailer rattling his keys to tease someone in custody. I'd invaded his sanctuary and now he had cut off my escape. I tried to remember what I knew about rattlesnakes. They are pit vipers, meaning they sense heat through openings in the nose. They usually don't strike if left alone. They hibernate from late fall to early spring.

Learn to think like your opponent, I'd been told by my football coach in high school. Anticipate his moves by seeing things from his point of view. But how could I imagine how a snake would think? For all I knew the snake was prepared to coil there at the top of the steps forever, and I would faint from lack of oxygen. Not daring to take the light off the snake, fearing it might come looping down the steps, I felt around with my feet for a large rock, something heavy to scare him.

The dust on the steps was deep, but my foot crunched on something that sounded like dry paper. I quickly turned the light in that direction and saw a mat of leaves and twigs. At some point years ago, this trash had blown or washed into the cave and lodged on the steps. In my pocket I had a waterproof container of matches. If I could light a mat of leaves and detritus and throw it at the snake, it might crawl away again. Were pit vipers afraid of fire? It seemed worth a try, for I couldn't think of other options.

Still holding the flashlight pointed at the snake with

my right hand, I stooped to pick up the mat with my left, hoping there were no spiders in the tangled leaves and twigs. A wad of the mat tore off in my hand and I stood again. But now came the hard part. How was I to reach into my pocket for the container of matches, take a match out of the tube, and strike it, light the tuft of debris and toss it onto the snake, while holding the flashlight? I dared not risk dropping the light.

The only possible way would be to place the flashlight under my right armpit, still aimed at the buzzing rattler, fish into my pocket for the canister of matches with my right hand, placing the canister in my left hand which held the mat of leaves, and unscrewing the cap. Taking out a match and placing the back end in my lips, I screwed the top back on and returned the tube to my pocket. Then with my thumbnail I struck the match and held it to the mesh of leaves and twigs.

Dropping the match, I transferred the burning mass to my right hand and grabbed the flashlight with my left, then raised myself to the next step. I'd always been told a rattlesnake can strike its full length. I was as close as I dared. As the flames touched my hand, I flung the burning detritus on top of the rattler. It hissed, uncoiled, and shot away. Climbing slowly to floor level, I shone the light around the cave and saw the rattler whipping toward the crevice it had sought before.

Desperate for fresh air, I found the tunnel and made my way out into the thicket of briars and vines. Sunlight sparkled through the canopy above, throwing nuggets of light on the forest floor. I felt like someone rescued from hell, or premature burial. I gulped the cool mountain air as one dying of thirst might guzzle water. Whatever I decided to do about the horror I'd seen below, I was now free in open air, with sunlight cutting through the beech trees.

Then I heard voices below me, men shouting with anger or fear. In the excitement of my discovery, and the stand-off with the rattlesnake, I'd forgotten about the bearded man. Had he returned? Had he brought someone with him? The tone of the voices suggested confrontation. As I listened I found the voices weren't coming from below, but along the base of the cliff, probably where the outlaw cave was, where the bearded man had likely been flopping at night.

Edging my way through the thicket of briars and vines, I followed the base of Devil's Courthouse to where I could see better. Staying hidden, I watched two uniformed men arguing with the bearded man who stood in the cave entrance pointing the pistol ahead of him. One of the uniformed men was the park ranger I'd seen before. The other appeared to be a North Carolina state trooper.

"Now, Wilbur, you'll feel a lot better if you put that gun down," the trooper said.

"I'll guarantee you nobody will hurt you," the ranger said.

"Ain't coming," the bearded man said. "I'm a free man."

The bearded man raised the pistol like he was going to fire at the ranger, but his hand shook.

"Now put that thing down," the trooper said. "You know you don't want to shoot anybody. You want to go back where you're safe, where you have a clean, warm bed, and people will help you."

"Won't go back," Wilbur said, lowering the gun.

"If you go with us we'll buy you a hamburger and French fries," the ranger said. "You must be starved up here. There's nothing to eat in these woods."

"I can kill a squirrel," Wilbur said.

"You're not going to kill a squirrel with that thing," the trooper said. "You couldn't hit a bear's ass with that monstrosity."

"Come with us and we'll get you a Co-cola, or a root beer," the ranger said.

"There's ghosts up here," the bearded man said. "I've heard them prowling around in the dark."

"Sure there's ghosts up here," the trooper said. "That's

why Indians called it Devil's Courthouse. You don't want to stay here another night. Put that gun down and come with us and we'll protect you from ghosts and panthers."

"The ghosts will follow me," Wilbur said. "Can't get away from them."

"Give us that pistol and we'll drive the ghosts away," the trooper said. "You won't see no more ghosts."

At that moment Wilbur's will and determination seemed to crumble, as if the talk of ghosts confused and unnerved him. He dropped the revolver in the dirt, and his face imploded, like a deflating balloon, and he began to cry. The trooper rushed forward and hit the afflicted man on the side of the head, knocking him into the leaves. The ranger kicked the pistol out of Wilbur's reach. Taking a pair of cuffs from his belt the trooper secured Wilbur's hands behind him.

With one on either side, the uniformed men raised Wilbur to his feet and escorted him down the slope, shackled and sobbing like a child who'd been whipped and humbled. There was something heartbreaking about what I'd witnessed. A disturbed person with a firearm was a danger, to himself as well as others. But it was painful to watch them break the man down, who'd only sought his freedom. And the trooper had no cause to hit him on the side of the head after he'd dropped the magnum.

I didn't move until the three men were out of sight and out of hearing. I had a lot to think about. Must I let the world know about the scene I'd witnessed deep inside the mountain? Or should I let those bones of the enslavers remain where they'd lain for almost five hundred years? The modern world had its own atrocities, more than enough. And yet I had a scientific duty to reveal what I'd seen, and let historians, the officials, archeologists, Cherokee authorities, know about the site. But would the Cherokees even want the world to learn about this secret? They must know about it, in stories passed down from generation to generation. If

I made public the scene in the mine, thousands might descend on it out of morbid curiosity, and looking for souvenirs. And maybe gold.

As I continued down the slope, savoring the fresh air, I had a lot of further thinking to do. For a while, anyway, I'd keep my discovery of the slave rebellion to myself. And gold was the least of my concerns.

When I reached the parking lot the patrolmen with their prisoner were gone. Only three sightseers remained, each texting on a cellphone.

BEYOND THE OUTER BANKS

When you're in a hurry all things conspire to frustrate you. I left work as early as I could to begin my two-week vacation, but Friday afternoon traffic in Raleigh was so bad it took several minutes just to get out of the parking garage to the street. And after that every light seemed to turn against me, as if they'd been waiting for my approach to go red. In July heat the air conditioning in the car was inadequate, and the air above the pavement boiled in conniptions of silvery mirage.

Caroline and the kids had gone to the beach house the week before. We'd rented a cottage right by the water on Ocracoke for a full month so they could enjoy a week of fun before I arrived, and a final week after I'd returned to work. But I was determined to make the most of my two weeks out of the office and reach the Outer Banks that night. I had to get out of Raleigh in time to catch the last ferry to the island, which left Swan Quarter at seven. That gave me less than three hours to reach the coast, and the line of cars and trucks backed up on the ramp to the expressway didn't help.

All I had to do was return to our house on the north side of town, make sure things like the water heater were turned off and windows locked, pack a few items from the fridge Caroline had asked me to bring, grab my bags, and I'd be off. Once on the beltway I passed everything in sight, swerving left and right as a race car driver would, glancing at the clock on the dashboard that ate minutes out of the sultry afternoon. There was heavy traffic far ahead as I could see, all of it pulsing and wobbling in dervishes of boiling air.

When I reached the house, I was surprised there was no mail, and then remembered I'd already had the mail held until I returned from Ocracoke. And I saw the burglar alarm was turned off as I walked into the living room.

"Damn it, who turned off the alarm," I said out loud.

Only then did I see an elderly woman standing beside the couch.

"Who are you?" I said.

"You don't recognize me?"

"No, I'm sorry. What are you doing here?"

I took out my cell phone to call 911. But the phone seemed to have been turned off.

"I'm Ethel Roberts, your ninth grade English teacher," the woman said.

I was so surprised I could only stammer, "How did you get in? I mean, what a surprise to see you. Won't you sit down?"

Mrs. Roberts sat down on the couch.

"You must be tired if you've traveled all the way from the western part of the state," I said. I looked at my watch. "What a shock to see you."

"I'm sure it is."

"Mrs. Roberts, I'm supposed to be at Swan Quarter by seven to catch the ferry. Otherwise I'd offer you something to drink."

"I know you must be in a hurry, Charles."

I looked at my watch again and tried to decide what to do.

"Would you like something to drink?" I said. "I'm not sure what there is. My wife and family are away at the beach and I'm supposed to join them."

"No thank you, I'm fine. I just wanted to visit with you a little."

My face grew hot with indecision. I could not be rude to this elderly woman who'd saved me once at a crucial moment in high school.

"I'm so grateful you didn't flunk me because of my poetry notebook, which I knew was a disaster." I said.

"But you wrote a fine paper on *The Call of the Wild*."

"I'll never forget that you gave me an A, Mrs. Roberts."

"You earned it, even though I knew you took some parts of that paper from *The Oxford Companion to American Literature*."

My face burned, and I hung my head. "I guess I did paraphrase certain passages. I'm sorry."

"That's OK. I knew you worked hard. You earned the A."

"Thank you."

"I saw you were not a quitter. After all the trouble with the poetry booklet you were willing to try again. That's what I wanted to tell you with the A. That's the most important lesson: always try again. You did well."

"Because you gave me an A, I was able to stay on the college track. And then I got a scholarship and was accepted for architecture school. Almost every good thing that has happened to me since can be traced back to your generosity, Mrs. Roberts. It was a miracle that you saved me."

"You saved yourself," Mrs. Roberts said.

"It's also a miracle that you're here now, that you came all this way from the mountains. What has it been, thirty years?"

"Thirty-two years."

"Yes, of course, it has been that long."

I had to look at my watch again. The precious minutes drained away, even as I tried to be polite.

"I'm very pleased to see you, Mrs. Roberts," I said, "But I really do need to run, if I'm to make that ferry by seven."

"You have plenty of time, Charles."

I glanced at my watch again, and put it to my ear. It didn't seem to be running.

"My watch seems to have stopped," I said. "Must be later than I thought."

"It's still early," Mrs. Roberts said.

"The dial says two minutes after four."

"They say time is relative."

"Yes, relative to the ferry that leaves for Ocracoke."

"There's someone else here who wants to see you," Mrs. Roberts said. She looked beyond me, and when I turned I saw a man standing on the other side of the room looking into a mirror over the buffet. I stepped in that direction, wondering why I hadn't spotted him before. He looked familiar.

"Uncle Alvin?" I said.

"Who did you expect? Albert Schweitzer?"

"I didn't expect to see you."

"Of course not," Alvin said.

"Where's Effie?"

"Probably somewhere in the back, stuffing herself. You know how she likes to eat."

"How did you get here?"

"We decided to take a little side-trip to see how you're doing. You staying out of trouble, Charlie boy?"

"I will be in trouble if I don't make the ferry to Ocracoke."

"What's the hurry, lad?"

"I'm sorry, but I was about to leave."

"All roads lead to the same place," Uncle Alvin said and laughed.

"I know, to the grave."

"That's right, son."

"Have you seen Mama and Daddy?"

"Not recently. I know your daddy's having problems with his heart."

"And Mama?"

"She's amazing. She takes care of him."

"I should visit them more often."

"Yes, you should."

"How did you get in? Did you come with Mrs. Roberts?"

"Yes, we arrived together."

"Why didn't you let me know? I could have planned to be here."

"This came up suddenly, you might say. Besides we all like surprises."

"Uncle Alvin, I really do have to go. Caroline and the kids are waiting for me."

"Have you met any big roosters lately?" Uncle Alvin asked.

"What is this about roosters?" Mrs. Roberts said.

"Go ahead, tell her," Uncle Alvin said.

I saw I had no choice but to summarize the story he'd reminded me of, as quickly as I could.

"When I was about three my family took me for Sunday dinner to Alvin and Effie's house. Alvin worked as a caretaker for one of the big estates in Flat Rock, called Sterling, a giant white columned house among pines with shaded lawns built in the 1830s. Effie was the housekeeper and Alvin looked after the lawns and shrubbery and did minor repairs on the house and out-buildings. There was a beautiful lake down the hill beyond the house and a stable for fine horses."

"You remember it well," Uncle Alvin said.

"Effie and Alvin lived in a small house set in the pines behind the big house. After dinner Alvin volunteered to show me around the estate while Mama and Effie cleared up and washed the dishes. I was delighted to get out of the house. Alvin led me to the goldfish pond where we threw crumbs to the fish. They churned and thrashed the water, fighting for bits of bread. I laughed and threw more crumbs.

"I'd never seen such a grand place as Sterling. The walkways ran under the trees and wind soughed in the pines. We wandered toward the lake which sparkled in the afternoon sun. There were swans on the lake and one swan raised its wing like a sail and careened across the water. It was not trying to fly, just skimming on the top of the lake. I was so thrilled by the sight I clapped. Next, we walked up the hill to the yard where chickens grazed and scratched the ground. There was only one rooster, flaming red, with blue tail feathers and long legs. It didn't seem afraid and stood in front of us, eyes blazing.

"Suddenly with a great thrashing of wings the rooster rose in the air flogging and fanning my face. Alvin jerked me back and I screamed and tried to get my breath. The rooster dropped to the ground and walked away with its feathers ruffled, like somebody who'd had a tantrum and was recovering their dignity. Mama and Effie and Daddy came running out the back door. It was only when Mama touched my neck and held up her hand that I saw the blood."

"Blood?" Mrs. Roberts said.

"I'd been so scared by the rooster's thrashing wings I hadn't felt it when he raked a spur across my throat. That's the way roosters fight, rising in the air and slashing with their spurs. If Alvin hadn't pulled me back when he did the spur would have slit my jugular. As it was, I had only a scratch across my throat. There was a little blood, but it was mostly fear I suffered. As Mama and Effie tried to calm me, Alvin got his .22 rifle and shot the rooster, then gave the bird to Mama to take home for supper."

"That's such a beautiful story," Mrs. Roberts said. "I can see how much you owe your uncle."

"Except for him, I wouldn't have lived past the age of three," I conceded.

"That's the best rooster we ever had," Uncle Alvin said. "Never got another half as good."

"I owe you," I said, and then looked at my watch.

"Maybe the ferry will wait for you," Uncle Alvin said.

"The ferry always leaves on time."

Uncle Alvin laughed. "Be sure you have a coin for the ferryman."

"I have a credit card; that should be enough."

"You never know. The rules may have changed. Can you carry a credit card in your mouth?"

Just then a woman walked in from the kitchen wearing a flowery sun-dress and white high-heels.

"Don't you recognize me, cousin?" she said.

"Of course I do." But she caught the uncertainty in my voice.

"I'm Brenda," she said. She put her hand behind my neck and kissed me on the cheek. I hugged her back.

"Charles is my kissing cousin," she said. "We were the devil when we were young. I could tell you some stories about the old days."

"What stories?" Mrs. Roberts said.

"Oh, about the time we played doctor in the back bedroom, and the time we filled our step-grandmother's panties with dirt where they hung on the clothesline."

"I really have to get going. I have to catch a ferry."

"But you just got here," Brenda said. "You have guests to entertain."

She turned toward the kitchen where more people were gathered. "Charles was always the shy one," she said. "Maybe I should tell them about the chocolate candy."

"If you must."

"Once when we were no more than four or five we were playing in our grandpa's house. Our parents had gone to hear Oral Roberts preach in Greenville, South Carolina, and they wouldn't be back until after dark. Our step-grandma had promised to bake cookies for us. But first she'd gone to the bedroom to lie down for a nap after clearing the table and washing the dinner dishes. Grandpa sat on the porch chewing tobacco and talking to his friend Cyrus.

"There were many places to explore in the old house, dark and mysterious and scary, closet, basement, pantry. But the scariest and best place of all was the attic. Though told not to go there, we loved to slip up the creaking stairs and pilfer.

"With no grownups watching we tiptoed up the steps, pausing and giggling if a board groaned. At the top of the flight the air was hot and dusty. In the light from the window, motes spun and wrestled like flocks of tiny sparrows. The air smelled with the tobacco leaves Grandpa hung from the rafters to cure. Magazines and jars were scattered on the floor. Charles saw something wrapped in bright tinfoil."

"'Look at this,' Charles said.

"'What is it?' I said.

"He picked up the foil and found brown crumbs like bits of chocolate.

"'It's candy,' he said.

"'No it ain't,' I said.

"'It smells like chocolate,' he said and held the package under my nose.

"'That's not chocolate,' I said.

"'I'll eat some to show you,' Charles said and picked up one of the moist pieces.

"'No you don't!,' I screamed and pushed the package away.

"'I'll eat it all myself,' Charles said.

"'You put that down,' I said and grabbed his wrist. And when he tried to pull away I smacked him. The tinfoil flew out of his hand and crumbs scattered over the attic floor.

"'Damn you!' Charles yelled.

"'You cussed,' I said. 'I'm going to tell on you.

"'Children!' a voice shouted. It was our step-grandma standing on the stairs, her head just above the floor level. Our shouts and bangs had awakened her. 'What are you doing?' she said. 'You know you're not supposed to play up here. There are wasp nests in the corners.'

"'She started it,' Charles said and pointed to me.

"That's when our step-grandma saw the tinfoil package and the crumbs scattered on the floor. 'My Lord, you didn't touch that, did you?' she said.

"'He tried to eat it,' I said proudly.

"'Come down from there this minute,' our step-grandma said.

"It was only when we reached the cooler living room that she told us the stuff in the tinfoil was rat poison. Grandpa had put it up there. She said if Charles had eaten the least bit he would have died. I enjoyed the look on his face when he realized what he'd almost done."

"Yes, you saved my life, and I'm grateful," I said.

"You're welcome."

I looked at my watch, and then looked around at all the company. "I appreciate this visit," I said. "You have all surprised me. But I really must be on my way."

"No need to hurry," Uncle Alvin said.

"You keep saying that! But the ferry leaves at seven. I'm late already."

"You're not late," Brenda said. "Look at your watch. Then again, maybe you're 'the late Charles Conway.'"

A woman with long black hair and bangs stepped out of the kitchen.

"My watch must have stopped," I said.

"Maybe you've abandoned time," the woman said. "You were always good at leaving things."

"Do I know you?" I said.

"Do you still like to play croquet?"

"Linda?" I said.

"I thought you might make some connection when I mentioned croquet."

"What are you doing here?"

"Just thought I'd drop in, while I was in the neighborhood."

"But you don't live in Raleigh."

"With modern travel, distance is not what it used to be. At least that's what they say."

"As I was saying, I really do have to go."

"I'm thrilled to see you too, Charles. You were always in a rush to get away, always in such a hurry. You might enjoy things more if you slowed down. You know, smell the daisies, before you push them up."

"But I'm already running behind. I have to get to Ocracoke this evening."

"I know how much you hate to let others down," Linda said.

"My family is expecting me."

Linda turned to the others gathered there. "Charles and I grew up as next-door neighbors. He was four years older so naturally I worshiped him. I followed him around like I was his assistant when I was ten or eleven. When we played hide and seek I hoped he would find me and pat me on the shoulders. When we played tag, I let him catch me so he'd touch me. I contrived to be where he'd notice me. I wrote in my diary about whatever he said and did."

"You were the prettiest girl in the neighborhood. When you started growing up you grew taller than the other girls."

"Yes, I started growing up, catching up with you. My family had a croquet set and there was a field between our houses that my daddy kept mowed. My sister and I set up the croquet set in the field and invited Charles to play with us."

"I think that's when I first discovered the love that led to golf."

"We played there on summer afternoons and Mother would bring us lemonade and cookies. The sun was bright, the grass was green. Charles liked to place his ball next to mine and drive my ball into the weeds or the ditch."

"That was part of the game."

"Of course it was. I liked to see our balls touching

before he knocked mine out of the field. Best of all were the lessons, when Charles stood close behind me and held my mallet to teach me how to swing. As he pressed against my back it felt like he was embracing me. I kept asking for his help in aiming the mallet."

"I remember especially your blue dress," I said. "Dark blue in the sun, and your long legs just getting hair on them."

"Every day I hoped the weather would be good so we could play croquet and you would stand behind me and show me how to hold my mallet."

"And I hoped there would be time after I finished work and took a shower to have another game on the grass."

"I loved it when we fought over something, when you grabbed my mallet and I tried to grab it back, and we wrestled and laughed. And then you went away to college, and we never played croquet again."

I looked at my watch. "Now I really must go," I said. "It's time; it's long past time."

"Einstein said time is an illusion," Linda said.

"Well space is no illusion. It's a long way from here to Swan Quarter."

"Yes, maybe farther than you think."

I shook the watch on my left wrist and looked at it closely. A distinguished-looking older man with silver hair and a colorful ascot stepped out of the kitchen and greeted me.

"Hello, Charles."

"What are you doing here?" I asked.

"I happened to be in this neighborhood and thought I'd drop in."

"But you've retired."

"Yes, I have."

"And moved to Boca Raton."

"Yes, I did, but a fellow has a right to return to see how his former colleagues are doing."

"Why would you want to do that?" I said testily.

"If you have nothing to do every day but play golf it gets kind of boring. Same old links, same clubhouse, same old jokes with the same old farts at the bar. You start to feel silly, spending so much time and money prodding a little ball into a hole in the grass."

I turned and spoke to those standing around me. "This is the guy who hired me right out of architecture school, and then tried to get me fired."

"Is that the way you remember it?" Algernon said.

"That's the way it was."

"Who do you think was your advocate at Gordon and Kennedy? Certainly not Mr. Kennedy."

"You supported me, at first."

"Yes, I did."

"And then you turned against me."

"Because I gave you a bad report?"

"Yes, damn it, you gave me a bad report, just when I needed your support."

"Why do you think I did that?"

"Because you turned against me. You were jealous."

"Jealous of what? Your failure to win clients?"

I addressed the others. "This is the man who almost wrecked my career."

"You were alienating clients, Charles."

"I was being honest with clients. I told them what was practical and what was not."

"And then they went to other firms."

"That was their choice, if they wanted fantasies instead of reality."

"You chased them away for no reason. You had to learn that an architect is as much a salesman as a designer. Without a client you can build nothing. You can draw castles in the sky at any time. To survive, you must persuade clients you can build what they dream of, yet design a structure that will be practical, and will last."

"Whatever you say, you turned against me."

"Listen, my friend, I saved your sorry bacon."

"With a report that almost got me fired?"

"You didn't get fired. I saw to that. You were young enough to think you were Christopher Wren and Frank Lloyd Wright combined. I brought you back to the real world." Algernon looked hard at me. "Were you fired?"

"I was put on probation."

"Kennedy wanted to sack you; so did Gordon."

"Because you gave me a bad report."

"Because you were losing clients. I couldn't hide that from Kennedy and Gordon.

"These were people who wanted buildings. It was your job to make them think their ideas and yours would complement each other, that you had practical solutions for their hopes and ambitions."

"When I was called on the carpet it was your report that Kennedy waved in my face."

"I wrote the report to save your ass, good buddy. I asked them to give you a second chance."

"You were jealous of a young architect with his own ideas, with balls."

Algernon shook his head and laughed. "Your generation always wants to make things sexual, and blame the 'generation gap.'"

"I'm talking about your report."

"Let me fill in some facts for you, young Charles. Let me put you and these good folks in the picture."

"You always had a way with words. You should have been a lawyer."

Algernon ignored my sarcasm. "You had lost three of our main clients with your stiff-necked more-artistic-than-thou attitude. Kennedy called a meeting of the board and said. 'That's three strikes for Conway and he's out.'"

"And you said, 'OUT!'"

"I begged him to give you another shot. I told him you were gifted but young. Your pencil was good but your salesmanship needed polishing. With a little experience you would learn to work with clients. Kennedy said we couldn't afford to lose another important client. But I persuaded him to let me write up a full report on your work and then give you another chance."

"And what was that?"

"You know very well what it was."

"You tell me."

"It was the water-works for the city," Algernon said.

"The board of commissioners wanted something Romanesque, something Henry Hobson Richardson might have designed a hundred years before. And I thought: this will be out of town, hidden by hills and trees, where almost nobody will ever see it. What difference will it make what it looks like? So I gave them what they wanted, with brick and heavy arches. And virtually no one will ever notice it."

"And the commissioners were pleased."

"They were. You'd have thought they designed that monstrosity themselves.

"It had a flavor of the traditional."

"Kennedy was pleased, for the city is one of our best clients."

"So that's why they kept me on?"

"And in four years made you a partner."

"I'm sorry that I snarled at you," I said.

"The young always resent their benefactors. They like to believe that they could have succeeded entirely on their own."

"I'm sorry." I looked at my watch. "But, really, I must go. I appreciate you all dropping in, but I'm already late."

"You know what they say," Algernon said, "all time is illusion."

I looked around at the people in the kitchen, and at some new arrivals. "What is this, a reunion?" I asked.

A stocky man in a flowery shirt stepped through the kitchen door. Thick gray hair bristled at his throat. "I guess you could call it that," he said.

"What are we celebrating?" I said.

"Can't you guess? Have you done latrine duty lately?"

I was startled by the word *latrine*. "Norwood, the drill sergeant, from Fort Hood?"

"I can see it's coming back to you."

"What are you doing here?"

"Just thought I'd stop by, while I was in these parts, so to speak," Norwood said.

"I am—surprised—to see you."

"Let's let bygones be bygones, run-off under the bridge."

"You disliked me because I'd been to college, and I was older than the other boys in the platoon. You were a fanatic, a god-damned lunatic."

"I did my job, college boy."

"I thought you were dead."

Norwood laughed. "Let's not take that attitude."

"It's just strange you should be here. You did everything in your power to make my days and nights in combat training a nightmare."

"That's what drill sergeants do."

I turned and spoke to the others. "He was like a character out of a movie, a cliché, a sadistic gung-ho torturer. It was a role he'd long ago perfected. He could have walked out of *Full Metal Jacket* or *From Here To Eternity*."

"I did my job."

"You singled me out for humiliation because I wasn't as afraid of you as the other recruits were."

"I was good at what I did."

"You made me do everything twice, whether it was crawl through a snake-infested mud hole or climb a rope or clean the latrine. Other recruits were grateful they weren't singled out for your abuse. They could see you were trying to get me busted out of Advanced Combat Training."

"It was for your own good."

I turned to speak to those standing behind me. "I was determined to show Norwood I could survive whatever he chose to dish out. I was in good shape at the time, had been on the track team in college, had run a marathon, gone through Basic Training with little trouble. But the Texas heat, the round-the-clock harassment, and lack of support from fellow trainees, began to tell. I started to wonder if I'd ever make it through after all."

"You were human like the rest, Conway."

"There was one August morning when we were called out for inspection just at sunup. Night hadn't cooled anything down. Even after showering and shaving I was sweaty. Sweat dripped off my forehead as I stood at attention. As Norwood worked his way down the line he bellowed something at every trainee. 'You look lost without your teddy bear!' he yelled at a boy named Jones. When he got to me he leaned so close his nose was an inch from my nose. 'Just look at that!' Norwood screamed and pointed to a damp spot on my chest where sweat had dripped. 'Your uniform is soiled, Conway!'"

"'Yes, sir!' I shouted, drawing myself to exaggerated attention.

"'Conway, you're a disgrace to this unit, and to me. While the rest of us go out in the field today to learn to be soldiers, you will clean the latrine with your toothbrush. And when you've finished that you will clean it again.'

"What I did I did thoroughly," Norwood bragged, and winked.

"'Yes, sir!' I barked. I knew that cleaning the latrine with a toothbrush was the oldest army punishment there was, going back at least to World War Two, or maybe even World War One. Choosing that as punishment was Norwood's way of showing his contempt. I wasn't even worth the effort of thinking up a new punishment. It was his way of suggesting I wasn't a major failure, just a minor screw-up."

"I was good at my job," Norwood said.

"So while the rest of the unit marched into the blazing sun with rifles and grenade launchers and packs of grenades to practice throwing and defense, I stayed back at the barracks with a bucket of soapy water, some rags and brushes, and, of course, my toothbrush. But soon as Norwood and the others were gone I put the toothbrush in my pocket and got on my knees to scour the concrete floor and walls and stinky areas around the commodes and urinals and sinks."

"You cheated," Norwood said.

I ignored the interruption. "To cheer myself up a little I thought about how cool it was on the floor, in the shade, out of the deadly Texas sun. Two trainees had died of heat stroke already that week. But it was hard to be cheerful. It was the separation and isolation from the platoon that hurt most. Norwood knew what he was doing, for I was alone."

"Damn right I knew what I was doing."

"The only real comfort in the army is the sense of belonging, the shared danger, the common hardships, the shared survival. I'd never felt so alone as I watched cockroaches scamper away into the dark corners of the latrine. I started counting them, but gave it up. A small snake whipped away and poured itself through the grid of a drain.

"As I scrubbed around one of the commodes I saw something taped to the back of the porcelain bowl. It was a little plastic bag filled with white powder. It was somebody's stash of cocaine or heroin. I decided I'd just leave it there. If I showed it to Norwood, he'd accuse me of abusing a controlled substance."

"Are you sure that wasn't your horse?" Norwood said.

"As I crawled and scrubbed cement in the dim light I began to see that Norwood was going to win."

"Of course I would win."

"He was holding all the cards, and I was not going to survive A.C.T. I'd go back and serve out my enlistment with other grunts, or maybe be discharged with dishonor."

"That's what I wanted you to think, good buddy. I had to destroy your presumed superiority."

"And then about the middle of the afternoon some of

our guys returned. When one named Evans, who everybody called 'Wichita' because he was from Kansas, saw me on my knees in the latrine he shouted, 'You lucky mother!'

"'Everybody can't be lucky,' I said. But when I looked up I saw blood on his camos. The other three guys had blood on their clothes too.

"'What happened?' I said.

"Wichita said Norwood had run them through brush and heat and dust until they could hardly stand. And then they had to crouch in a ditch and throw grenades at wooden targets thirty yards away."

"Twenty-five yards away," Norwood said.

"In the dust and sweat it was hard to even see the targets. They pulled the pins and threw as hard as they could. Norwood walked behind them yelling in their ears."

"Motivation. Standard procedure," Norwood said.

"When it was Jones's turn and Norwood screamed, 'Pitch the pineapple, you pussy!'"

"I always liked the sound of that," Norwood said.

"Jones pulled the pin and started to throw, but must have suffered a heat stroke at that instant because his legs gave way and he sank into the ditch with the safety lever released."

"He was a loser. I could see that from the beginning. It was my job to get rid of him."

"Somebody tried to grab the weapon still in Jones's hand, but the grenade rolled away, and it was like everybody froze for a second, and then all rushed to grab the grenade but they collided, and nobody could grasp it. In the movies a buddy always seizes the loose grenade and throws it away, or covers it with his body to save his buddies. But this was not the movies."

"You're telling it real good," Norwood said.

"Because of the heat and fatigue and Norwood's screaming, no one seemed able to think quickly. Wichita and a few others backed away, but the explosion caught most of the rest, and fragments set off other grenades on their belts and in boxes in the ditch."

"It was a bloody mess," Norwood said.

"I could hear sirens and helicopters in the distance. Wichita sat on a bench and cried."

"It was just an accident," Norwood said.

I turned to Norwood. "You saved my life in that latrine."

"Guess I did at that," Norwood said and grinned.

"Thank you."

"You're welcome."

I looked at my watch in confusion. "Now wait a minute," I said to Norwood. "You're supposed to be dead. You were killed with the others."

"There you go, using that word again," Norwood said.

I turned, facing the crowd, for I'd just remembered something astonishing. "And Brenda died of breast cancer when she was thirty-seven. And Uncle Alvin died of heart failure. And Mrs. Roberts lived into her nineties but finally succumbed to old age. And Linda was killed in a car crash on the Asheville expressway."

I walked to the kitchen door and looked out, and saw a large group around the pool and the children's swing set. All were smiling at me.

"Why are you all here?" I said.

A man in a well-tailored suit stepped forward. "We're here to welcome you," he said.

"Do I know you?"

"You probably don't recognize me. I'm Tim McDowell, the banker who caught the clerk embezzling from your account when you were in college. Had he succeeded in cleaning out your account you'd have been forced to drop out of school."

"Thank you. But why are you here welcoming me? This is my house."

"It looks like your house," McDowell said. "It's less shocking if you feel you're in familiar surroundings."

"What do you mean?"

A young man with a beard stepped forward and said, "Perhaps this poem will help you understand."

"Who are you?"

"I edited the literary magazine at the university. I'm Lester."

"I heard you died of a drug overdose in San Francisco, long ago."

"Don't believe all you hear."

"I don't," I said.

"This poem is by Gary Snyder," Lester said.

"I remember you. Your name is Lester Gregory. You took LSD."

"That's me, chromosome-damaged Lester. I wanted to open the doors of perception, as we said in those days."

"You dropped out of school."

"The school dropped me. I had other educational interests to pursue."

"I'm sorry. I have a ferry to catch. I'm late already."

"Yes, you are 'late' already. But the ferry will wait."

"The ferry does not wait."

"Do you want to hear the poem or not?"

"Maybe at another time."

"This is the perfect time," Lester said and began to read. "Ko-san and I stood on a point by a cliff, over a rock-walled canyon. Ko said, 'Now we have come to where we die.' I asked him, what's up there, then— meaning the further mountains.

'That's the world after death...'"

"Are you trying to tell me I'm dead," I interrupted.

"We prefer not to use that word," Mr. McDowell said.

"Is there a better word?" I said.

A man wearing overalls and a baseball cap walked up to me at that moment. His hands clutched the bib of the overalls. "Hello, Charles," he said.

"Hello."

"I wanted to see if you'd still speak to me after going off to college and becoming a big shot architect in Raleigh and winning prizes."

"Do I know you?"

"Do you remember losing a pocketknife?"

"My daddy gave me a pocketknife for my twelfth birthday, but then it disappeared."

"That's right."

"It was stolen by a boy named David. Later I saw him playing with the knife in the classroom."

"That's true; you did."

"Are you David?"

"Right again."

"When I accused you, you grew indignant, said your grandpa had given you the knife."

"That's what I said. It was a lie. I'm sorry."

"That knife was my delight. It was my twelfth birthday present. How did you get it?"

"You left it on your desk while you went to the bathroom, or something. Maybe you went to the principal's office to use the intercom."

"That's right. The principal let me use the intercom to make announcements."

"We were all jealous of you because you got to use the intercom. You also ran the movie projector when the school watched movies."

"I was a little older than the other students in the class."

"You were the teacher's pet. Admit it. We all hated you."

"Hated me?"

"Let's just say we resented you."

"Is that why you stole my knife?"

"No, I wanted that knife. It was such a fine knife, a grownup knife."

"Yes, it had brown bone handles and a plaque on one side that said 'Case.'"

"And a flare on the handle that helped to grip it."

"Did you enjoy keeping my knife?"

"I did, or at least I told myself I did. Which is almost the same thing when you're a kid. But I also lived in fear that you'd take it back, or steal it back."

"I half-believed you when you said your grandpa gave it to you."

"But you knew I'd taken it; you accused me of taking it."

"I had no proof."

"Where would I have gotten such an expensive knife, exactly the same as yours? You were too timid to claim it."

"I half wanted to believe you, that your grandpa had given you the knife. I had merely lost mine. It seemed safer that way."

"So you forgot about it."

"In effect, I guess I did. And the next summer I bought myself a smaller knife, a cheaper knife."

"And you cut yourself badly. You ran with the knife open, and fell on it."

"How do you know that?"

"We all know, here."

"That's strange. I'd almost forgotten that incident. When I fell, the knife cut my chest."

"If you'd had the bigger knife it would have stabbed into your heart."

"So you're suggesting you saved my life by stealing my knife."

"It's possible. In fact it's likely."

"So I owe you a lot for stealing my knife."

"We could put it that way."

"So I should thank you? I do thank you."

"Forgiveness is enough."

At that point a heavy-set man with a red face came forward and shook my hand. He wore a suit and tie. "Hello, Charlie, and welcome," he said.

"Do I know you?"

"I'm Preacher Bob. Don't you remember my tent revival?"

I shivered with astonishment. "I do, way back when I was twelve or thirteen."

"You got saved at my revival that summer."

"You had a tent with a sawdust floor in the field at the edge of town. The loudspeakers were so loud we could hear your voice a mile away."

"And the singing, all the wonderful singing. Make a joyful noise."

I studied Preacher Bob, and said, "May I ask what you're doing here?"

"I thought that had been explained."

"Everybody tells me I don't need to worry about a thing, about catching the Ocracoke ferry, which I must have missed by now."

"But you have passed over, Charles."

"Over to what?"

"Over here, with us."

"But this is my own house, with my own backyard. And I have to catch the ferry to Ocracoke." I looked at my watch yet again. "Why has my watch stopped?"

Preacher Bob ignored my question.

"So tell me again what you and the others are doing here?"

Mr. McDowell stepped forward. "Let me show you something," he said to me.

Mr. McDowell led me around the corner of the house just as the paperboy passed on his bicycle and threw a paper into the yard. The banker picked up the paper and read the headline: "'Local Architect Charles Conway Killed in Car Crash on Beltway.' Is that your picture, name, and address?"

"What happened?"

"It says here you were hit by an eighteen-wheeler. You never saw it coming as you wove in and out of lanes on the expressway. You passed instantly."

"But I made it back to my house, back to here."

"That's the way it seemed," Mr. McDowell said.

"You mean I'm not at my house?"

"You are and you aren't."

"What does that mean?"

"It means you have crossed over."

"Where is my family? Are they OK?"

"They're safe on Ocracoke Island," Mrs. Roberts said.

"Do they know what's happened?"

"Not yet, but they will in a few more minutes of earth time."

"What can I do to comfort them?"

"We can't interfere with those left behind," Mrs. Roberts said.

"What about Mama and Daddy?"

"There will be others to comfort them, neighbors, ministers, relatives."

I looked around and saw more people arriving in the backyard. They were coming from all directions. A white Greek temple was visible on the hill beyond the yard. Some of the people I recognized, and many I had forgotten. All had touched my life in some way.

"Each person here has saved your life at some point," Mr. McDowell said. "That's why they've come, to welcome you."

I was overwhelmed by the number of people gathered and arriving. "In Sartre's play he says, 'Hell is other people,'" I said.

"What did Sartre know? After all, he hadn't been here, then."

"I wonder if the opposite could be true, that heaven is other people?" I said.

"Let's not jump from one extreme to the other," Mr. McDowell said.

"Then where is this place?" I asked.

"Let's just say it is," Mr. McDowell said. "Do we need to characterize it more than that?"

"I'd like to know where I am."

"You are with all those gone before who've touched your life," Mr. McDowell said. "That is the reality. You are, and you are with them. Is that not enough?"

"I am?"

"You are on a stage, and in a stage of transition. To be is to be in transition. We are always in transition. We're here to help you. It's easier if there are familiar folks, and familiar surroundings. Look at all the well-known faces."

I looked around slowly and nodded with recognition.

"You're here with us now," Mrs. Roberts said. "You can't get lost."

"What do I have to do?"

"Just showing up is enough, that and your curiosity. And you will help to welcome others. Would you like that? This is only the beginning, of another kind of journey. It will take you a little farther than the Outer Banks."

Linda came forward and took my arm. "I always knew we would meet again," she said.

I hesitated before answering, "Well, since I have no choice I might as well volunteer."

Everyone in the crowd laughed, including Norwood, who laughed loudest. "I'll make you a good damned soldier yet," he said.

JUDACULLA ROCK

Having been raised on a farm in the mountains of western North Carolina, in the Old North State, Jim Evans had known Judaculla Rock since childhood. It was a large boulder of soapstone, partly exposed above ground in Jackson County, on Caney Fork Creek, just off Highway 107. The visible surface of the rock was inscribed with figures—petroglyphs, they are called. When he studied North Carolina history in the eighth grade there was a photograph of the rock in the textbook. The markings resembled graffiti and chicken tracks.

The textbook explained that the Cherokees, who lived and hunted in the vast ranges of the Blue Ridge and Unaka Mountains, must have drawn a map on the stone of their great victory over the Creeks at Taliwa in 1755. That battle had been fought in North Georgia, and the Creeks, perennial enemies of the Cherokees, had been defeated so badly they withdrew their villages farther south, away from Cherokee land. The hero of that battle was Nanyi'hi, later called Nancy Ward, last War Woman of the Cherokees. To Jim, in the eighth grade, that seemed a plausible explanation of the figures on the rock. However, the textbook added that some anthropologists and historians disputed that interpretation, yet conceded they did not really know how to decipher the petroglyphs.

In high school, Jim fell in love with biology, with microscopes, dissection, and the glorious narrative of evolution as paralleled in embryology. Compared to the fundamentalist Baptist theology drilled into him from infancy, science was the good news, opening the door to other concepts of time and meaning, inspiring him to explore history and ideas. An earth billions of years old seemed far more exciting than a world only six thousand years old, created intact and static. People had said to him: the loss of faith must have been painful and wrenching for you. But Jim's answer was that he did not lose his faith, only expanded his view to include all of creation, from the atoms to the amoeba, to history, and to the farthest stars.

At Chapel Hill, Jim considered studying medicine, but loved botany so much he went on to pursue a doctorate, writing a dissertation on ferns and club mosses of the Piedmont and mountain region of the state. Hired by a small Lutheran college near the middle of North Carolina, he gave most of his career to teaching biology to future doctors and nurses. And for an interval he even taught geology, after the professor of that subject retired, and the college couldn't afford to replace him. Over the years, Jim published a number of books and papers on club mosses and ferns, and the effects of climate change on gametophytes and ground pine, on plants that reproduce by spores.

After he retired, and his wife Lisa, who was a nurse, also retired, and their three children married and moved away, Jim finally had the time for field work that he'd missed while teaching. Now he could go out and look for ferns and club mosses whenever he chose. As a boy he'd gathered ground pine, which was called "turkey's paw," for Christmas decorations. With his new freedom he considered expanding his research to include some saprophytes, especially the rare and beautiful Indian Pipe.

An article in the Charlotte newspaper made Jim think of Judaculla Rock again. The reporter said that someone had vandalized the stone, chipping away markings with a hammer. A young man had been arrested, and claimed in court that he'd been directed to destroy the figures on the soapstone by God. The pictures had been carved by beings from outer space, from beyond the known stars, who had invaded the planet long before people existed. The petroglyphs foretold the bad things that had happened on earth, the wars and plagues, the Holocaust, 9/11, and the doom of the human race. Only destruction of the terrible signs of prophecy could save the planet from further tragedy.

The lawyer appointed to defend the young man argued that his client had been high on drugs and suffered from acute paranoia. Besides methamphetamines, the young man had smoked marijuana and taken LSD and fentanyl. The lawyer appealed to the court to send his client to rehab, not to the penitentiary.

But the story of vandalism was not the most interesting part of the article. The reporter had done his research. He'd gone back to James Mooney's classic, *Myths of the Cherokees*, and found that Judaculla was a slant-eyed giant, Tsul kalu, who lived at Kanuga on the Pigeon River. The giant fell in love with a girl in the valley, and each time he jumped from the rock to the valley below to visit his lover, he left a mark on the soapstone. The markings were the record of the pursuit of his beloved.

The most arresting feature of the article came last. A local high school teacher of biology had looked at the figures on Judaculla Rock and claimed they were the shapes of microscopic animals. There were amoebae, paramecia, diatoms, rotifers, flagellates, and many other protozoa and chrysophytes. Since none of these living things could be seen with the naked eye, whoever drew them must have had some means of magnification. The teacher speculated that the carvers of the shapes might have had microscopes, or possibly natural microscopic vision.

The reporter had also interviewed several archeologists who'd studied Judaculla Rock and two other, smaller, soapstone boulders in the area, and discovered that the petroglyphs were much too old to have been made by Cherokees. The Cherokees had only been in North Carolina for eight or nine hundred years; their language showed that they were closely related to the Iroquois of Upstate New York. Whoever made the figures on Judaculla Rock had belonged to one of the earlier Woodland Tribes, now lost to history. In fact, one archeologist even speculated that the markings predated the Woodland period, and belonged to some unknown era in the peopling of North America. In Cherokee legends, the pictures on Judaculla Rock had often been ascribed to some earlier inhabitants of the region.

Jim was stunned by the article, and he re-read it several times. As a scientist he was skeptical of much of the content. It sounded too romantic, like a story by H. P. Lovecraft about giants and monsters who inhabited the earth long before humans evolved, and who might still be hidden deep in the planet's interior or under the ocean. And he knew there was a tendency to romanticize anything to do with Native Americans. But the opinion that the carvings represented microscopic organisms was too fascinating to pass up. He went online and googled Judaculla Rock and the local teacher.

"Of course this is all absurd," Jim told Lisa. "The microscope was not invented by Leeuwenhoek until the seventeenth century."

But Jim couldn't put out of his mind the image of prehistoric beings who somehow had microscopic vision, chiseling what they could see on Judaculla Rock to show to anyone in broad daylight the minute life all around them.

That night he dreamed a kind of movie in which the article he'd read got mixed up with a horror story about vandals from beyond the stars who brought to earth the seeds and spores of life. They destroyed much that was already on the earth and planted amoebae, diatoms, and algae, to start the evolutionary process all over again. And to record their visit they drew on stones the images of the life they'd brought, so that descendants through the ages would know how their ancestors appeared. The petroglyphs were the work of giants, giants so large that even human beings were no more than amoebae to them, so powerful they could fly through inter-galactic space. In the dream, he knew he was dreaming. But he also understood that as a scientist, a specialist in spores, it was his duty to study the signs left on Judaculla Rock for clues about the makers of the pictures, and their meaning. It was a wonderful dream, a scary dream that left him exhilarated and exhausted. He felt called, like Peter the fisherman, like Saul on the road to Damascas, like Moses at the Burning Bush. He remembered the black monoliths in the film *2001: A Space Odyssey*, markers placed to lead evolving humans toward the wonders and wisdom beyond deep space and time. Jim woke laughing at himself, and at the intensity of the dream.

He knew well it was just a dream, but he also understood that he would have to visit Judaculla Rock, have a firsthand look at the markings. Of course, he didn't believe prehistoric beings had microscopic vision, but a visit to the rock would give him an excuse to see his native mountains again, and maybe look for some rare species of ferns known to survive in remote coves and hollows of Jackson County.

"Let's take a little trip," he said to Lisa at breakfast. "We could visit Highlands, Cullowhee, and the Smokies."

But Lisa protested she had her garden club, her bridge

club, and her work as a volunteer for the Friends of the
Library book sale. "They're your mountains," she said.
"Go back and savor your old stomping ground. Who
knows, you might run into an old girlfriend, or find
some rubies in the Cowee Valley."

Jim had always found it hard to explain the exuberance
that came to him when driving west from the Piedmont,
back into the mountains. He'd left the hardscrabble farm
years ago, but still felt a rawness in his throat when he
glimpsed the blue wall of the Blue Ridge rearing ahead,
especially in summer, when the hill country was boiling
and the mountains stretched cool and fresh against the
sky. A thrill seized him as he saw peak behind peak
rising ahead and began the climb to higher elevations.
In part, it was the spirit of returning home, back to the
high valleys where he was born and grew up, where as a
boy he delighted in Indian Pipes, ironweed, lady slipper,
where he found arrowheads in the fields and swam in
the river on the hottest days. But it was a spiritual élan
also, a euphoria, as he spotted an old church almost
hidden in a cove, a waterfall at the head of a valley, a
railroad winding through a deep ravine.

When Jim first left the mountains for college, the
two highways to the east were US 70 and 64. Both
wound round and round off the highlands. His uncle
used to joke that the fellow who built those roads hung
himself because he couldn't put another curve in them.
But the new Interstate swept up in a long arc out of
the Piedmont, through deep cuts in the ridges, soaring
over streams and hollows, gliding into the highlands so
smoothly that only the popping of your ears reminds
you that you're gaining elevation. As you swing around
grand curves, the scenery takes your breath: deep valleys
with tiny houses and roads far below, ridge above ridge
ahead, so distant they appear to merge with the clouds.

Except today, the sunlight of the Piedmont gave
way to overcast as he drove west, and by the time he

passed Asheville the highway was buried in fog. It was impossible to see cars and trucks a hundred feet ahead. The fog was white and ghost-like, a million tiny mirrors or opals reflecting headlights. He slowed and felt his way along the Interstate, hoping no eighteen-wheeler would flatten him from behind.

At Waynesville, Jim turned onto Highway 23, now also a four-lane route, which took him to Sylva. As the road mounted higher he prayed to finally get above the fog. But instead of thinning, the mist pressed ever closer against the windshield. It felt as if he was driving into a cellar or under water. Signs were impossible to read until he was even with them. He regretted he'd picked this day for the excursion, though he knew full well that fogs are common in these mountains in any season, including summer.

As he turned onto highway 107 the fog seemed worse yet. The vapor pushing against the windshield boiled in crazy turbulence, chaotic, as though riled by frantic winds. It was only by luck that Jim saw the sign for Judaculla Rock, now a historic site, a kind of park, and he followed the arrows to a small empty parking area. As disappointed as he was by the weather, he was relieved there would be few others out sight-seeing. He'd have the site to himself. He could take as much time as he needed.

The park service had built a kind of viewing platform beside the rock, and a sign told visitors to stay on the path and on the platform, and not to touch the rock itself. But with vapors swirling around him, Jim could hardly see the boulder from the deck. He stepped carefully off the platform and approached the rock. Bending closer, squatting beside the stone, he could see that the grooves in the soapstone had been lined with chalk to make the figures stand out.

He understood quickly that whoever said they were drawings of one-celled animals highly magnified had been joking. Instead he saw stick-like figures, some

human and child-like, drawings that might be fish
skeletons, and octopuses with eight long legs. There
were sun-bursts and half-moons, filigree, and what
might be crabs. And perhaps letters of some archaic
alphabet. And he saw the place where a hammer had
destroyed some of the figures.

At first Jim was disappointed, for he'd loved the story
of prehistoric beings who drew microscopic life. But
then he saw that the untranslatable mystery was even
more exciting and appropriate. The markings were like
the deep language of nature itself, dark energy, black
holes, and dark matter, like the strange attractor, the
first cause: elusive, essentially unknowable. The more
we know about nature the less we understand. That's
why science is so thrilling. We always look for the key
that unlocks the code, the semiotics of our world, that
recedes the closer we study. These ancient scriveners had
understood and inscribed that very sense of mystery.

If he'd had to hazard a guess there in the fog, he
would have said the figures represented some ancient
map of the zodiac, or zodiacs, mythological figures
imposed on the stars and planets. And others, coming
later, could not resist making their marks also, turning
the map of the heavens into a palimpsest of graffiti,
filling up the available spaces between the earlier signs.

As Jim bent over the glyphs, pleased with his
thoughts and speculations, he became aware that he
was not alone. Someone stood beside and above him.
He'd been concentrating so hard on the markings he'd
not heard them approach. He saw dirty pink sneakers
and bare legs with scabs like fleabites. Startled, he said,
as calmly as he could, "Excuse me, I didn't see you."

"Mister, you've got to help us!" an urgent voice gasped,
a woman's voice.

He pushed himself up and saw a woman taller than
him. Her blonde hair was unkempt and her face pale
and not too clean.

"How can I help?" Jim said.

"It's my daddy. I think he's had a heart attack."

"Where is he?"

"Just down the trail there," the woman said breathlessly. "We was hiking and he got sick and passed out. Please come help." The woman pulled at his arm; she seemed desperate.

He should have taken out his phone then and called 911. That would have been the logical thing to do, if someone had really had a heart attack on a mountain trail. But Jim was surprised and distracted by the churning fog, disoriented by his meditation on the petroglyphs. The urgency and apparent panic in the woman's voice couldn't be ignored. She drew him toward the woods and he stumbled after her.

Even in the rush it occurred to Jim the woman didn't look like somebody who would be out hiking and camping in the foggy weather. It was not only her accent, but her clothes. Her shorts and blouse looked cheap and dirty. People who hike and camp in the mountains usually wear heavy socks and walking shoes, khaki shorts and shirts with many pockets. This woman's clothes looked like cast-offs.

"How far is it?" Jim said.

"Just down the trail a ways." Her voice had a smoker's rasp. "I think he may already be dead," she added.

"I'm not a doctor," he said. "At least not that kind of doctor."

"Please, mister, you've got to help us."

The fog in the woods was so thick it was hard to see the ground. Trees loomed out of nowhere, and branches slapped at his face. He stumbled on a rock or log.

"We've got to hurry," she said.

If only he'd stopped to call 911. But she kept pressing him to go faster. And he wouldn't know what to tell the First Responders until he'd actually seen her father. They walked on and on in the fog and came to a rhododendron thicket, where she stopped.

"Where is he?" Jim said.

"Right in there," the woman said and pointed under a bush.

As Jim stooped to look he became aware that someone else had stepped up behind him. A stick snapped, and then he didn't know anything.

When he woke in cold wet leaves Jim saw the fog around, thick as before. His thoughts, too, were deep in shadow and slow to focus. The back of his head throbbed. He was cold, and when he felt around he found he was completely naked. Even his shoes were gone. His phone, wallet, car keys, all had been taken. He sat up under the rhododendron bushes and tried to think. Slowly the events came back to him, the visit to Judaculla Rock, the girl in the fog, the story that her daddy was dying, the long walk through the woods. He'd been taken in by the most obvious con. The clues that the woman had been lying were obvious in retrospect, yet he'd gone along like a moron.

Jim's next thought was that no one must ever know how he'd been tricked. He must conceal his stupidity, his naivete. And slowly it began to sink in just what a mess he was in. His wallet was gone, his money, his credit cards. His identification. And maybe worst of all was that he had no clothes. Even if he found his way out of the woods, what could he do? Flag down a car on the highway? Who would stop for a crazy man in his birthday suit waving his arms? Vanity was the least of his problems.

His best hope was to somehow get arrested, then explain things to the cops. But in the deep fog, how was he to find someone to arrest him? Jim realized it had been hard to follow the trail with the woman because there had been no trail. She'd said there was a trail and he'd believed her. She'd led him deep into pathless woods, into a rhododendron thicket, what used to be called a laurel hell. He was lost.

Jim pushed himself up and held onto a tree. Often

in his life he'd contemplated what he'd do in such a desperate fix. Would he panic and act like a fool? Would he bravely and calmly assess the challenges and meet them? Would he prove to be a coward, or a resourceful survivor? It would do no good to kick himself. Jim knew the mountains were now overrun with crime, crackheads, drug pushers, burglary rings, scam artists of all kinds. But studying the petroglyphs had seemed to be a rational and worthwhile venture.

Think! he said to himself. Until you have a plan stay right where you are. He recalled a line he'd read in a poem once, "When lost in the woods, let the wilderness find you." But that seemed a little silly now, just the kind of paradoxical statement poets, safe in their studies, like to make.

As he stood in the fog, in the wet leaves, holding onto the sapling, it seemed the bottom had dropped out of the world. He'd not felt such despair since he was a graduate student and was told his fellowship would not be renewed. He was naked and utterly alone, and knew he'd acted like a sucker. The fog was smothering.

To distract himself in his youth he'd repeated the question that we most of the time avoid: what is the explanation of it all? What is the very essence, what is the logic of our lives, and of the universe that we know? It can't be just endlessly reproducing ourselves.

While pondering these happy verities, Jim clutched the sapling. The fog was getting thicker, if that was possible. He could hardly see the rhododendron leaves nearby. Was his vision failing? Had the strength of the blow to his head damaged the optic nerves? And then it came to him that the day was waning. It must be getting dark. He had no idea how long he'd been unconscious. His watch had been taken. His glasses had been taken. In the fog it seemed that time did not exist.

Look for moss on the north side, the Boy Scout Manual used to say. He vaguely recalled the woman had led him in a northerly direction from the clearing

around Judaculla Rock. So, if he could determine what
way was north, he should go in the opposite direction.

But in the fog and dim light Jim could see no moss
on the saplings or on anything else. Touching the trunks
around him, he felt nothing that seemed soft and padded
like moss. It was at that moment that he panicked and
did exactly what all folklore, all Scout Manuals, and the
poet, warned him not to do. He started running, with his
hands out front to push away limbs. He stumbled over
rocks and logs and picked himself up. Limbs slapped
his face and twigs lashed his eyes and ears. His knees
grew weak and he tripped and fell in the wet leaves, his
shoulder thudding against a large tree trunk.

Jim cried. He didn't have the willpower any longer
to think deep, dark thoughts about the meaning of life,
or the lack of meaning. That was a luxury for the safe
and spoiled. He was too weak and helpless to be ironic
or cynical. He cried like a child lost from his mother,
no longer able to laugh at himself or be sarcastic. He
wept and sat, leaning against a tree, and eventually he
became drowsy with exhaustion and slept.

In his dreams Jim imagined that his naked body was
a stove and he fueled his stove-body with willpower
and imagination. It was a matter of concentration. He
burned his thoughts for fuel. In the dream his mind
turned back to the designs on Judaculla Rock. It didn't
matter who had made the markings. The meaning
was the same, whoever had done the carvings, and
whenever they were scratched. The petroglyphs showed
the clutter, the confusion, the ambiguities of human
consciousness. They were a graffiti wall, a bathroom
wall, of fragments where many had left a mark, drawn a
picture, told a story, come to leave a signature, a motto,
a sign of belief or disbelief. The rock was a ledger of the
perennial human aspiration to make sense of things, to
leave a legacy, even if only a confession of uncertainty.
For some ancient people, the Rock was their internet
and archive, their social media, where they left messages

for each other, and for posterity. It was their history
the way the wampum belts were a record for the later
tribes. Because the Cherokees did not know how to
read the pictures, they speculated that the slant-eyed
giant Judaculla had marked the soapstone as he leapt
into the valley below.

When Jim woke it was still foggy. He'd not eaten
or drunk anything since yesterday morning. Moisture
gathered all around him, clinging to his skin, but he
couldn't drink the fog. Luckily it was summer, or he
would have died of exposure in his nakedness, at that
high elevation. He was as naked as Cabeza de Vaca
when he returned to Mexico. He might have crawled on
all fours to eat grass like Nebuchadnezzar, if he could
have found any grass.

If you walk downhill you will come to a stream, to
the headwaters of a stream, he told himself. If you come
to a stream you can drink. If you follow the stream it
will lead you to a larger stream, and that stream will
lead you to roads, to people. In his nakedness Jim did
not know how he would be received. But he knew he
had to find others. Only other people could help him.

He tried to discern which way the ground sloped.
Feeling with his feet, holding onto trees and limbs, he
descended, or imagined he descended, through the woods.

In the fog Jim didn't see a spring, or even smell it, but
felt the wetness with his feet, and found he was standing
in wet leaves accumulated in a catchment. Dropping to
his knees, he pushed away leaves and sticks and muck,
and saw that indeed there was a little pool. He'd made
the water muddy, but there was a ripple of ebullition as
the water emerged from an opening in the rocks. He'd
found a spring. He waited a few moments for the little
basin to clear, and cupped his hands and drank.

What a difference a drink of cold, fresh water can
make! Jim didn't know how thirsty he was until he
gulped the spring water that had seeped through veins
inside the mountain. For him it was better than the

elixir of the alchemists, or the fountain of youth Ponce de Leon searched for in Florida. He splashed water on his face, and on his shoulders and chest. He was covered with dirt, leaf bits, twigs, cobwebs, scratches. He was lucky he hadn't been bitten by a black widow spider or a copperhead.

It was while washing himself in the cold spring water that he noticed a fern on the bank below the spring. In the fog it was hard to guess at first what species it was. But as he looked closer he saw it was a Common Rockcap, a fern that grows on top of rocks and feeds on decaying vegetable matter. Related to the Resurrection fern, but not epiphytic, *Polypodium Virginianum*. The blades on the fronds look separate and symmetrical, but in fact are joined and alternating. In his dissertation he'd devoted several pages to the Rockcap and its range in the Piedmont and mountains. It prefers shady acid soil but can thrive on boulders and cliffs, if there is enough moisture. Spores are borne under the blades near the tips of the fronds. They grow best where there is little sun.

As Jim searched farther he found other ferns, not a glade exactly, but a slightly more open space, with Royal and Cinnamon ferns, Rattlesnake and Hay-scented ferns. Their lush fronds curved in the fog like giant feathers. He thought of monks in medieval scriptoria writing fancy letters in books of history and theology. The green fronds loomed gray and silver in the mist. He thought he saw a rare Goldie's Giant fern and stepped closer to get a better look.

But it was not a fern that startled him. Two brown legs stood behind the Goldie's Giant. Jim jerked back, and then looked up at a small person in a white shirt. He couldn't tell at first if it was a boy or girl. He covered his crotch, remembering his shameful nakedness. Could this be one of those who robbed him, returned to kill the only witness to their crime?

"Who are you?" Jim said.

The person, tall as his chest, didn't answer.

"I've been robbed," he said. "And they took all my clothes."

The figure remained silent, and Jim looked closer to make sure there was really someone there. It occurred to him he might be hallucinating from hunger, or from stress and fear. He was sixty-seven years old, and he'd never been so scared and lost. The person in the white shirt had a dark face and dark hair.

"I can explain why I don't have any clothes," he said.

Still the figure watched him without speaking.

It was almost certainly a boy, with black hair and black eyes, watching Jim as though curious, as if he wondered whether Jim was human or a ghost, or some alien being, or maybe a lunatic.

"I won't hurt you," Jim said. "I just need to find my way out of here. Can you tell me who you are? Do you know how we can get to the nearest road?"

Jim might as well have been speaking to one of the ferns. As mist swirled around his face he felt dizzy, as if vertigo was coming on. The boy was still as a carved statue. His eyes did not move or blink. Jim thought he might be ten or eleven. It was hard to tell. He tried to think who the boy might be. His skin was dark as a Mexican's. He knew there were thousands of Hispanics living in western North Carolina. Most worked in the fields and in construction. Maybe this boy was a recent arrival who didn't understand English. Jim tried to think of some Spanish phrases.

"Per favor," he said.

Still the boy didn't speak. There was something about his face that didn't seem Mexican. It was thin and angular. His silence unnerved Jim, the staring at his nakedness. He'd never felt so ashamed, for he'd brought all this ludicrous misery on himself. Guilt and helplessness overwhelmed him and a sob choked his throat and heaved his chest. Jim wept without meaning to, and wiped his nose and eyes with the back of his hand.

Jim had a PhD, was a scientist, a professor emeritus. He had a wife and children and grandchildren. He'd published books and many articles in peer-reviewed journals, and he belonged to a number of professional organizations and learned societies. He had a pension. But none of that could help him. The boy in the shorts and long white shirt watched him wipe his eyes and said nothing. It occurred to Jim he might be a deaf-mute.

Then the boy turned away. He gestured for Jim to follow. Jim hesitated. Would he lead him into a trap? Did he work for the drug traffickers, the meth sellers? But what trap could be worse than the one Jim was already in? What choice did he have? The boy paused and looked back and gestured again, and this time Jim followed.

The boy picked his way among ferns and boulders, and then away from the stream through the trees. As they walked, the fog seemed to thin a little. Jim realized he could see the boy clearly, and farther into the woods ahead. The boy took his time, making sure Jim was able to tag along. His brown legs and sneakers made hardly a sound on the wet leaves. Jim stayed five or six feet behind him.

As he walked Jim decided the boy might be an Indian, a Cherokee. The Qualla Reservation was only twenty-five or thirty miles to the north, on the Oconaluftee River. But as they wound around trees and crossed logs Jim thought of a story he'd grown up hearing, about a so-called will-o'-the-wisp, a spirit that came to someone lost or injured in the woods and led them to safety. The will-o'-the-wisp was usually described as a light that floated ahead of the lost person. But this boy was no will-o'-the-wisp. He didn't speak, but Jim was pretty sure he was no ghost.

Jim heard a hawk whistle. Shafts of sunlight shot through the canopy above and threw spotlights on the leaves. The air was getting warmer. They passed the ruins of what looked like an old moonshine still. Jim's uncles had made moonshine when he was a boy, and one, Uncle Harry, had served a year in the Atlanta penitentiary for selling blockade whiskey.

Jim's feet were sore, but he didn't dare drop behind the silent boy serving as his scout and pilot. The word scout made something click in his head. He recalled that early explorers of the region, men such as Daniel Boone, found people who lived in the woods like Indians, but were not Indians. They were dark people with mostly Caucasian features, called Melungeons. Scholars over the years had studied them, to learn their language and where they might have come from. In the early days, some had described them as the Lost Tribe of Israel, while others declared them to be Welsh people who'd come to the New World before Columbus. Others said they might be descended from Sir Walter Raleigh's Lost Colony, who had wandered into the wilderness from the east coast in the 1580s and intermarried with the Indians.

But more recent scholars had determined that the Melungeons were part Turkish and part Cherokee, with some African blood. The boy who was leading him could be a Melungeon. Given his dark skin, his slim figure and features, Jim was pretty sure that's what he was.

"Where are we going?" Jim called. But the boy kept walking and didn't answer. Jim was almost certain he could hear him. Once, the boy looked back to confirm that Jim was still following, and then he resumed his pace.

"I'm grateful that you're helping me," Jim said, but the boy didn't respond.

The fog had cleared away and blue sky was visible above the treetops. The sun was so bright it blinded him. And then he heard voices, not loud enough for him to distinguish words, human voices calling to each other.

"Wait!" Jim called to the boy. He stopped and thought the boy must have heard the voices too. Jim pointed. "There's someone there!"

When he looked again the boy was gone, vanished into the trees as quickly as if he had been beamed away in a sci-fi movie.

"Where are you?" Jim called.

The approaching voices grew louder. And when two

hounds on leashes and a deputy sheriff in uniform and
half a dozen other men broke through the underbrush,
Jim cringed and covered his naked crotch, relieved and
ashamed.

"I was robbed," he said to the deputy. Jim told him
his name.

"We know, Dr. Evans," the deputy said. "We've
been looking for you."

The deputy carried a pair of coveralls, the kind garage mechanics used to wear, and Jim put them on. The
deputy had no shoes for Jim's sore feet, but he did have a
bottle of water and several energy bars. As Jim munched
the bars the deputy told him his clothes had been found
in his car, which had been driven south and abandoned
in Georgia. Lisa had informed the police he was visiting
Judaculla Rock. Now she was on her way to Sylva to
look for him. The deputy said Jim could call her on his
phone.

The people who'd mugged Jim had made dozens
of purchases with his credit cards in North Carolina
and Georgia. And they'd not yet been caught. The
deputy said he was sure they'd targeted other visitors
to Judaculla Rock. A sign should be put up warning
people not to go there alone.

"People keep going up there hoping to figure out
those scratches," the deputy said. "But I could tell them
they don't mean a thing. Just a bunch of doodles."

Jim could see why the deputy would say that. But
he knew the deputy was wrong. The carved figures told
a profound story, about the need to tell a story, to all
who would care to look or listen.

"I'm awfully glad to see you folks," Jim said to the
deputy and his companions. "I'm grateful you came
looking for me. You and this boy have saved my life."

"I don't see no boy," the deputy said.

Jim turned around to look again for the boy in the
white shirt, but the woods behind him were empty.

THE SECRET FACE

What he saw at first appeared to be a light-colored rock in the pool at the bend of the stream scooped out of the riverbed. The water was far from clear after spring rains, and Tony wasn't sure he'd seen anything. He re-baited the hook and threw it farther out to wash to the lower end of the pool where trout would be feeding. His dad had taught him to let his bait float down for trout to snap up. With no rod, only a pole, he had to fling the line by hand to splash and sink at just the right spot to catch the current and not get stuck in the back-spin of the eddy. Then he would stick the rear end of the pole in the bank and watch the line fret, waiting for it to go tight. As he waited, he counted the seconds up to a hundred, then began counting again.

In late April the new filbert leaves, touched by sun, gleamed like candles with green flames. There was a scent in the air, a fragrance he couldn't name, that came from a certain blossom, maybe a vine. It was the smell of the river at that time of year, associated with the

murmur of the rain-swollen stream and breeze in the
trees, and calls of nesting birds. If luck was with him,
the scent of trout would be added to that of the river,
and sweetness of the blossoms.

Before he sat down by the pole, Tony noticed the
white object in the pool again. It could be a rock or
something man-made dropped in the river upstream.
There were farms in the valley above, and things got
washed or thrown into the current. Once he'd seen a
dead calf caught on a rock in the shoals further down.
He'd also found a broken doll, a crushed guitar, a
deflated volley ball, and a dead cat.

Something about this object made him step to the
edge to look closer. With a jolt, he recognized eyes
and hair troubled by the spin of the eddy. To see
better, he leaned forward and indeed made out eyes
and a mouth. Tony jerked away and glanced toward
the sunny pastures above the river and trees stirred by
the breeze. For seconds he refused to turn back to the
water, but listened to crows in the pines beyond the
pasture, a truck climbing on the gravel road toward
Cedar Springs. An airplane crossed far above, probably
the flight his dad called The Chicago Delta. He waited
a full minute before turning back to the pool.

Just then the pole began to twitch and bend. He
pulled the shaft out of the ground and felt a trembling
as the tip whipped back and forth. The line was taut as
a mandolin string and zipped through the water with a
scalding hiss. He slowly lifted the pole as the line raced
to the left and to the right, ahead, and back. The pole
arced with weight as he lifted the line out of the pool,
and a rainbow trout bright as silver set with tiny prisms
flogged the surface. Quick, before it could throw the
hook, he swung the fish onto the bank where it thrashed
in weeds and grass. The trout had swallowed the hook,
and it took him several attempts to pull the line free.

To keep the catch alive and fresh, he broke a forked
stick from a sweet shrub, ran one prong through a gill,

and stuck both ends in the sand beside the water. This trout was about a foot long, maybe thirteen inches. His mama would cook it for supper. With fumbling fingers, he threaded a new worm on the hook and flung it back into the channel at just the right spot. To calm himself, he began counting again. Counting was a kind of charm, and if he counted slow, and long enough, another trout would take the bait, maybe a mate of the one just caught. The river, the air and light, his counting, must cooperate for luck to hold.

Only then did he remember the thing in the water that looked like a face. When he turned that way it was still there. The eyes stared. In the *National Geographic Magazine* he'd seen the heads of marble statues from ancient Rome or Greece with eyes wide and staring. He bent closer: these were not marble eyes, but real. He fancied they were blue, and fixed on him. Tony looked away, then back. A ripple made the eyes seem to wink, and the mouth appeared to move as though speaking. He shuddered. The eyes followed him.

As his eyes adjusted to the depth, he found a body attached to the head, hard to distinguish because the clothes were sprinkled with sand and mud. Something about the face and shoulders told him it was a man. The hair was short. He could see no arms, and wondered if the hands were tied behind the body. The head lifted and sank, prodded by the current, the way a boat tied to a dock will shift.

As he studied the face, Tony wondered if he could recognize the features. Was this someone he knew? Or was it just a big doll dressed up, the kind in department store windows to model suits and shirts. Such a doll had a name: mannikin? a tailor's dummy? Did mannikins have blue eyes? The river water was dingy, what his dad called "dish water," perfect for catching trout, but it made him question his eyesight.

The face bobbed, and the ripple seemed to shatter the features into pieces, then let them fuse again. The head rocked as if nodding, staring through two feet of water. The features appeared familiar, then not familiar, drifting closer, receding. The lips were distorted, as though screaming, then closed.

Tony knew he must report what he'd seen to grownups. They would tell the sheriff and other authorities, maybe the preacher. There might be issues of law and crime. Could he be held responsible for what he'd discovered in the backwater of the fishing hole? It was his duty to let people know, to inform adults. And yet, why not wait a while? This was his discovery. No one else knew what he'd found. Maybe it was all a trick, just a mannikin, a model, a big puppet washed into the river upstream and trapped by the pool. Why let others know immediately? He could study the face and decide what it meant. Tony had heard of moonshiners killing informants and dumping bodies in water. There must be a story behind what he'd found. It surprised him that he was so reluctant to disclose what he'd discovered. He sat on the bank and examined the face that appeared to blink and speak, and then freeze. He almost heard the voice, among the sounds of the river, birds, and breeze.

When he was younger, Tony had enjoyed fishing. From the time he was five or six, if fields were too wet for work, especially in the spring, his dad would tell him to get a can out of the trash. There was a place below the hog-pen where every shovel of dirt yielded a dozen or more worms, small red worms, wigglers that writhed in contortions, long nightcrawlers with threads like screws, worms with swollen blisters in their middles. Dad dug in the rich soil and Tony gathered bait in the can.

With poles over their shoulders they marched along the trail by the river, climbed a hill above the stream, and as soon as they crossed a bluff heard the roar of the falls on Bob's Creek. They fished in a deep hole where the creek entered the river, throwing their hooks far out into the stream beyond the revolving pool, then waited for a strike. Once when they caught three foot-long rainbows, Dad cleaned the catch with his knife, made a fire, and cooked the fish on sticks beside the river. The smell of the river suggested anticipation, surprise.

It was in the spring when he was twelve that Tony's enthusiasm for fishing soared to a new level, in early April, the beginning of trout season. While in town he bought a license, a black fishing line, a bag of hooks and sinkers. Soon as he reached home he cut a pole from a maple sprout, wound the line on the tip, and headed for the river. The trees were just beginning to bud, but the air retained a chill. It had been raining, and the water was dingy, but not muddy. From the can he took a long worm and impaled it on a number-four hook, squeezed a sinker on, unwound the line from the end of the pole, and threw the bait into the current. He began to count as he waited, and hoped that if he caught one trout he might snag another, for trout were supposed to travel in pairs that time of year.

When the tip of the pole jerked, he lifted the shaft, expecting a pulsing pull. But the jolt was harder than he'd ever felt before. Had he hooked a mud turtle? Was the hook caught on a log? He raised the pole a little, and suddenly the line went crazy, throbbing and jerking, then tore away, slicing the cloudy water so fast it whistled, swung around near the head of the pool, and returned. The string cut through water with such speed it sounded like it was burning. Round and round the hole it crackled. The pole was almost jerked out of his hands.

Tony knew he was supposed to set the hook with a firm yank, but it was all he could do to hold onto the pole. He walked back and forth on the bank, following the line, hoping the string wouldn't break. His arms shook so he could hardly grasp the pole. Let it play, he whispered to himself. Let it play. That was the advice in the fishing stories he'd read. Wait for a trout to tire itself. His feet kicked up dirt and rocks and trampled weeds as he followed the line.

Finally, he decided it was time to haul the fish out of the water, and risk breaking the pole or line. With trembling hands, he lifted, and the surface exploded, with thrashing, flashing, slapping, tail-dancing. With a heave he swung the pole and landed the fish in the weeds. Before the catch could leap back into the water, he grabbed it with both hands, clutching the slick, scaly sides.

It was not a rainbow, but covered with spots like jewels, a German Brown, hardest of all trout to capture. It was the biggest and fattest trout he'd seen. The prize flopped and writhed, almost too strong to hold. The hook had been swallowed, too deep to be extracted. He cut the line and attached another hook and sinker. If he was quick he might capture the mate. With hands so unsteady he trembled, trying to slide on a worm. When he finally got the hook in the river he began to count. The trophy fish stirred in the weeds. But he got no other bites.

At home his dad measured the fish: seventeen inches. Mama fried the prize for supper. After that day, Tony hurried to the river every afternoon, between school and milking time. He fished the river and Bob's Creek, every pool and shoal, every riffle. Fishing became his rage, a passion. In church, in school, while feeding chickens, he thought of fishing. He bought new hooks and sinkers, and planned, when he had enough money, to purchase a rod and reel, and maybe dry flies, like a real fisherman. Fishing was a vocation, a calling. Water was a place of mystery, and fishing a gamble, more addictive than poker or dice.

Tony caught a number of fish that spring, ten or twelve inches long, for eating. But he never took another one like the German Brown.

He never told his parents or anyone about the body in the river. He meant to, but kept putting it off. It was his duty to reveal the secret, but he couldn't. The awful fact must be hidden from other eyes. He felt guilty for keeping the discovery to himself, but if he told anyone he could be accused of waiting too long and maybe punished. Was it a crime to find a corpse and not report it? There must be a law against what he'd done, or not done. Still, he couldn't bring himself to tell. If he told, his wonderful, terrible, personal secret would be forfeited.

Most days he came back to the same pool to fish, and stared at the face among the rocks. He couldn't look away from the visage, even as the cheeks grew ragged, as if eaten by small fish or other creatures. Once he saw a crawfish resting on the mouth. And then a worm crawled out of an eye. Minnows entered the nose and flitted out.

About a week after finding the corpse, Tony was surprised while fishing by his friend Roger. Roger was a cousin, and they'd known each other since their earliest memories. They'd dammed ponds together on the branch, played ball in the pasture, explored gullies, rolled rocks off mountaintops, slid on boards downhill in snow. But now Tony didn't want to fish with anybody else, not even Roger.

"Your mama told me where to find you," Roger said. He'd brought his own pole and can of worms and bag of hooks and sinkers. Tony stood near the body in the water, hoping Roger wouldn't notice it. Roger wasn't an avid fisherman, but he'd brought a bag of cookies to munch, and he offered one to Tony. They sat on the bank eating cookies and watching their poles.

"Ain't no fish here," Tony said

"Then why are you here?"

Tony told him this was where he'd caught the big German Brown, but never another one. "I keep hoping."

If Roger noticed the white object in the pool, he must divert him, get him away.

"Let's try down the river," Tony said.

"But I just got here."

"This hole is fished out."

Roger stood and looked in the direction of the body. "What is that white thing in the water?"

"Just a white rock, I reckon."

Tony lifted his pole and pulled the line out of the water.

"What's the big hurry?"

"I'm sick of this place," Tony said.

A few days later a big Buick stopped beside Tony as he carried his pole to the river. The driver rolled down the window and shook ash off a cigarette. "Hey, buddy," the man called, and motioned for Tony to come closer. "You like fishing?"

"Yeah," Tony said. "I caught a big one this spring."

"I like fishing too," the man said; he looked so hard into Tony's eyes it made him nervous. He'd never seen the man before, and wanted to go on.

"You see anything unusual in the river?" the man said.

"Like what?" Tony looked up the road and down the road.

"You fish in the river a lot?"

"Yeah."

"Have you seen anything surprising?"

"No, sir."

"If you was to tell what you'd seen you could be in trouble."

Tony looked down the road, hoping another car or truck would come. "Ain't seen nothing."

"Just remember what I told you." The man knocked more ash from his cigarette. "You wouldn't want no trouble."

"No, sir."

The man drove away in the long car.

That afternoon Tony threw his line into the far side of the pool and sat on the bank counting. The body in the water had moved a little, and the head appeared to shake. The color of the face had changed from white to blue-green. More bites had been taken out of the cheeks. The mouth was opened wider, and minnows swam in and out. The head bobbed, moved by nudges from the splash of the river.

It puzzled him that he'd told no one about the body, not even Mama and Dad. It was his privileged secret, his private knowledge, not to be shared. To tell would betray himself, and put him in jeopardy. The man in the car had threatened. Could he himself be blamed for the death somehow?

The secret was also a kind of wealth, a luxury he couldn't explain. It was like hoarding a treasure, a hidden asset. He'd never kept such a thrilling secret before. Knowing about the face in the water would only be bad if someone else discovered it. If the mystery was revealed he would have nothing, less than nothing. He would be blamed. As he waited he counted to a hundred twice.

Tony cringed to remember the way the man in the big car had searched his eyes, like he knew Tony was lying. The man must know something about the body. But why would he leave the corpse there to be found, unless he didn't know where the body was? The man's accusing stare made the air taste like broken glass.

At least Roger hadn't looked closer and actually recognized the head and body. If Roger had told, Tony would have had to pretend he thought the head was just a rock in the water. What was the penalty for not reporting a body? Was it a crime to conceal a crime?

The tip of the pole jerked, and Tony lifted it out of the dirt. As the line circled in the pool he felt a trembling on the tip. The line above the water blurred like a banjo string. A rainbow would swing around and pull. Whatever it was on the hook vibrated, fluttered. He raised the quivering weight out of the water, and the fish fanned the surface, flinging spray. He swung the catch into the weeds and watched it flap and dance.

The fish had orange spots decorating its sides, coins of different colors. As it trembled, sand stuck to its skin; the gills stretched for more oxygen. When he picked it up to extract the hook, it almost jumped out of his hand. Suddenly Tony knew what he'd taken: a native speckled trout, the kind that lived in the streams when settlers arrived years ago. His dad had talked about catching speckled trout, brook trout, when he was a boy. Speckled trout lived in small, cold streams near the headwaters. Brook trout had vanished when the rainbows and German Browns had been introduced in the river, retreating to pure streams higher in the valleys.

This trout was more than eleven inches long. It was no trophy, yet in a way it was a trophy, simply because the brookies were thought to be gone from the river. Dad would be pleased to see the native fish. And speckled trout made good eating.

As he freed the hook from the lip and thought of cleaning it to eat, Tony glanced at the face in the pool. The corpse had been there for weeks. The water in the pool must be contaminated with dead human flesh. The fish in his hands had swum in such water. The speckled trout was pretty as a piece of art from an ancient world, set with garnets, amber, rubies, and stones he didn't know the names of. Yet, what kind of germs must be inside the flesh? He dropped the hook and heaved the unusual catch back into the river.

There was a saying that creek water will clean itself, running through rocks and moss, in a few hundred yards. But this water had circled over the body, not flowing over rocks, nor filtered by moss. Instead of tossing his hook back into the current, Tony sat down to think. The lips of the face moved, like they were pleading with him. But it was just the minnows. It was said the dead sometimes speak to the living, but what could this body say? A ghost would be in the air, in shadows, transparent, thin as vapor. A ghost would come in the night and touch its victim.

Tony had heard in church about the dead rising at the end of time, called forth from earth and ocean. But this body was in neither earth nor ocean. And it was not the end of time. Or could it be the end of time? He tried to imagine such an event: He listened, thought he heard no birds, not even crows in the pines on the hill. Water murmured faintly, but there was no other sound. Trees didn't move. The air was dead, as though time had stopped and he'd been left behind. That was what preachers predicted, that bad people would be left, after good people got taken up to heaven. The moon would turn to blood. Sinners would cry out for mountains to fall on them. There would be gnashing of teeth. Time had died and he'd been abandoned, while all he knew had been taken away. He must be the last living person, if he was alive, or in some other state. For not telling about the corpse, he was guilty as a murderer, and now he was paying for his negligence, as time had come to an end.

The shift-whistle at the cotton mill blew. He'd always considered it a shrill, ugly sound. But now it was a joyful noise, for the whistle suggested the world still went about its business and time had not stopped, but plodded ahead in the usual way. He could breathe again, drink the seconds like cool air. The afternoon opened out with possibility.

Tony sat, but didn't re-bait his hook, or stir. He heard the birds again; a car crunched on the gravel road. It was as though a switch had been thrown, and things restarted.

Maybe it was a splash or gulping sound that drew his attention to the river. Shoes rose out of the water and then knees in brown cloth. Slowly a torso floated to the surface. The head began to lift off the rocks and bob to the top, features eaten, one eye socket empty, the other eye staring through a strand of moss. The head nodded as ripples rocked it. Without touching his pole, Tony dashed up the bank and through the hazelnut bushes.

Three days later Tony returned to the fishing hole for his pole and bag of hooks and sinkers. As he parted the limbs of the filbert bushes and descended the bank he

tried not to look into the pool where the corpse had
risen as if on Easter morning. But once he reached the
water's edge he couldn't help himself. However awful
the face might be, he had to confront it. More than a
test of his courage, it was a duty. He owed it to the
body as a witness. He'd kept his vigil and his secret
for days, weeks. The body had given him company. He
owed the dead a measure of regard.

But as he gazed into the pool, Tony found only sunlight
reflected from the surface. Spots coming through the trees
danced and stretched in dips and ripples. He stepped to
the left to see better into the pool, but spied only rocks
on the bottom. There were sparks on the water farther
from the bank, but he found no face or features.

Tony sat in the weeds, both relieved and disappointed,
as though waiting for something, but there was only
the muttering of the river, and crows in the distance.
Something was supposed to happen. He waited and
felt alone. The corpse in its bizarre way had been his
friend, his secret companion. No one else had known,
nor ever would know. He'd been deserted, orphaned.
After waiting a long time, he picked up the fishing pole.
To his surprise, the worms in the can were still moist,
alive. Distracted, he slipped a worm on the hook and
flung it into the current.

That night his dad read aloud a story from the
newspaper, about a body found in the lake further
down the river.

"Yesterday a body was discovered in Lake Pinnacle
floating in deep water near the dam. The flesh was
badly decomposed, but the coroner found items in the
clothes identifying the body as one Eliot Smathers of
Greenville, South Carolina, who has a record of arrests
for drug trafficking. Mr. Smathers was last seen on
April 29th.

"According to the sheriff's office, and a report from
the State Police, law enforcement believes Smathers was
killed in a dispute over narcotic sales and distribution.

His body had been buried in a shallow grave found near the headwaters of the river, and floods from recent rains washed it out and downstream.

"Mr. Smathers was part of a drug ring operating out of Atlanta. No charges have been brought, pending further investigation."

After he heard the story from the paper, Tony considered telling his parents about the body he'd studied so many times. It could be a kind of bragging, to reveal that he'd known about the corpse all along, weeks before it had been spotted in the lake. But how could he explain not telling anybody?

Every time he returned to the fishing hole Tony looked into the pool, as if expecting to see the head, lips appearing to speak when stirred by the current. Each time he glanced, in spite of himself, but knowing better, let down that there was nothing to see. The pool was empty, even when he caught a fish to take home.

One day in late May when he returned to the river, he noticed the water was in deep shadow, because the trees above were fully leaved. It was a different place from the site in early spring when trees were just beginning to show green. There had been an openness then, scented with new flowers. Now the smell of mud was strong. Soon school would be out and work in the fields would begin, with no time for fishing. He stared into the pool where his line hung limp and lazy.

Steps thudded on the bank behind him, and Roger emerged from the rows of filbert bushes, carrying a pole and a brown paper bag. "Thought I'd find you here," he said.

"Fish ain't biting," Tony said.

Roger unrolled the line from the tip of his pole and spindled a grasshopper on the hook before tossing it into the river. The bag he'd brought gave off a honeyed aroma.

"Do you want a doughnut?" Roger said. "Mama brought me a dozen from town."

IN THE
SNOWBIRD MOUNTAINS

What woke me sounded like a long grunt, then a knock, and something breaking away. I grabbed the flashlight and checked my watch: just after 2AM. A wild boar would not be rooting around at that hour. In the Snowbird Mountains the only things to fear were boars and feeding bears. My supplies hung on a limb out of reach of prowling beasts. I'd picked the Snowbird Mountains in Graham County because fewer tourists came there than to the Smokies, and fewer bears were used to feeding on garbage. Maybe I'd dreamed the sound.

But the growl came again, louder, with popping and snarling, too powerful to be from any known animal. Unzipping the sleeping bag, still half asleep, I couldn't imagine what was happening. As I crawled into the open and shone the light around, everything appeared as it was at bedtime, oak trees nearby, my grub hanging from a limb in a waterproof bag, charcoal from my fire.

The racket grew on the mountain above, like the

ridge was tearing loose. Trees must be breaking, rocks crumbling, all in a long vomit of gushing soil. It was a landslide or mudslide headed my way in the dark. The ground quivered so much I lost my balance and fell over. I couldn't run, and I couldn't even hobble with my cane fast enough, trapped, with the shoulder of the peak plunging toward me. It was one of those moments, as in a nightmare, or when your car begins to skid on ice, or you fall off a high ladder, when you know your days may be at an end. My whole life didn't flash before me, as they say in books it's supposed to, but I did have a glittering thought, that, Oh, this is how the adventure will end.

In what direction could I have run? I couldn't even remember where I'd placed my cane, in the tent or outside? My boots were in the tent. Whatever was happening on the mountainside was crashing closer by the second. I didn't even try to brace myself for the avalanche that would bury me. Wind, pushed by the wall of mud and debris, stirred trees nearby. It would be hard to dig me out of the falling debris.

Rains the week before, day after day, three inches some days, had flooded rivers and creeks. I'd put off my camping trip because of the storms, one following another. Tornadoes had chewed up houses and mobile homes, brought power outages, highways closed. Soon as the rains stopped, my wife Lois drove me to Graham County and left me at a trail head. With my pack and walking stick, I climbed as far back in the mountains as I could reach before dark.

As the roar grew, I wondered if I'd see what would kill and bury me. But nothing hit, as if the cataclysm had changed course, off to my right. Turning the flashlight that way, I saw an ugly tongue of broken trees, boulders, and mud tall as a locomotive, streaming by a few rods away. Rocks slammed trees and mud leap-frogged itself, but my little tent and I were spared. The mess kept rolling, a giant spill oozing cold lava, guts from hell.

There are no terms for describing my relief. With sheer luck I'd placed my tent just out of the mudslide's path, as though a guarding hand had guided me. I'd come that near to my end. The slide was so close I smelled roots and tree sap, broken rocks, mud, soil not exposed to air since the planet was young. The thick gush of spoil slowed but didn't stop. When daylight came I would examine the gash made on the mountainside.

Something banged on the trees above, sounding like a loose rock, but before I could think of getting out of the way, my leg was hit, my good left leg, so hard I fell. I'd not felt pain like that since my first seizure a year before. When you have a seizure your first thought is to control it, but of course you can't. The agony takes control of you. You are its puppet, its plaything. The pain is so sharp the brain refuses to process it. I knew what had happened: a rock, loosened by the slide, had rolled down the mountain, glancing off trees, and hit my left leg below the knee. And then I didn't know anything for a while.

The year before I'd had surgery to remove a meningioma. When I strolled into the hospital early that morning in June I didn't know I'd never walk normally again. After surgery, as sensation returned to my limbs I found I couldn't move my right leg below the knee. The motor control there was gone, though I could feel a touch on my ankle and foot.

The rock that broke my left leg lay beside the tent. I found I couldn't stand; my right leg would not support me. I crawled to the tent and found my cane, but holding the stick I still couldn't raise myself. The right leg trembled and buckled. I tried again, and fell again.

Troy, old boy, you're in a fix, I whispered. You're stranded far back in the mountains. I sat, trying to think. There is always a solution if you're lucky enough, or smart enough, to find it. To walk to the campsite with the pack had been labor enough, with the cane in my right hand. I'd hiked several miles from the trail to reach the pure solitude of the woods and mountains, by a stream murmuring over rocks. Even if I could get to the trail I'd still have four or five miles to the parking area where Lois had left me. But on the trail there might be other hikers to help.

The mobile phone was in my backpack, but it was out of range of any tower. Only closer to the highway would the phone be usable. How far could I crawl before the device would connect? Unable to stand, I couldn't recover the bag of supplies. There would be nothing to eat until I saw other human beings. Maybe with a rock I could kill a small animal, though standing up was impossible. Surely somebody would find me. When I made another fire, I'd send up smoke and a plane would spot it. I'd place my tent in the open to be visible. A ranger helicopter would locate me. I must remain calm. There was the creek nearby, and it was possible to go without grub for days or even weeks in moderate weather.

There was the awful pain in the left leg that I could do nothing about, except try to ignore it. Tylenol was in the bag hung from the tree. The ranger helicopter came over at least once a day. If it was bear or boar hunting season there would be hunters with dogs in the mountains. But this was mid-summer, and the only hunters would be poachers, determined to stay out of sight.

I pulled my jacket from the tent and wiggled into it, already shivery with mountain cold and with pain. The smartest thing would be to crawl back into the tent and wait for dawn. I could think clearer in daylight. I switched off the flashlight to save batteries. Only then did the stars shine brighter beyond the trees and over the line of the ridge, calm and far away from my pain and fear.

When I placed a hand at my side to steady myself, the palm touched water. There had been no puddle there before, and no rain since I arrived. I reached out to find the depth of the pool and my knee sank in cold water. Switching on the flashlight, I saw muddy water, spreading far as the light could reach. There was a sizable body of water where there had been only the creek before, and it was rising.

My first thought was that a flash flood had converged off the slopes above and was pouring down the valley. I'd need to get out of its way. Except this water was not rushing, but stretched level across the ground, covered with floating debris and sticks. And then I knew what had happened: the landslide had dammed the creek and the stream was rising as a pond or lake. I had to get out or I'd be drowned. Even as I considered my peril, the icy water soaked my knees and calves. In a few minutes the tent would be under water. I grabbed the sleeping bag with my right hand and pulled it from the tent. There was no direction to go except away from the brimming water, up the slope. Holding the flashlight in my left hand and the sleeping bag in my right I began to crawl, grinding knees on rocks, sticks, picking a way around trees and knocking my head on limbs. The boots were back in the tent. The flashlight fell out of my hand and rolled down the slope. I let it go.

Crawling like Nebuchadnezzar, I thought. I'd been raised in a Baptist church. Would I end up on my belly, eating grass with the kine, like the king of Babylon? Moving under the circumstances fast as I could, I left all my supplies, tent, extra clothes, cane, binoculars, behind. Hands and arms and knees were cut by briars and sharp branches. Twigs raked my eyes and ears. Cobwebs stuck in my hair.

An animal ran away in the leaves ahead. I paused, but didn't hear it again. On my knees and elbows, I was vulnerable to rattlesnakes and copperheads, black widow spiders, not to mention bears and wild boars. This time of year there were sting worms in the woods, called packsaddles, as well as hornets, hickory wasps, and honey bees. I was on the ground with rabid squirrels, raccoons, and vulnerable to deerflies and other blood-sucking insects.

Wrestling upward, dragging the sleeping bag, I finally dropped with exhaustion, unable to move further. I rolled onto the sleeping bag, and looked at the stars beyond the trees. My head was in a fog: what had happened to me seemed unimaginable. I'd sought the peacefulness of the woods and landed in Hades instead. It was my first venture into the woods since surgery. I'd been near death in the hospital, but had survived and learned to walk again. Was this the end I'd struggled for? Had death been postponed, only to seize me in the mountains I loved?

As I lay on the bag looking at the chaste stars and attempting to ignore the pain in my leg, an odd thought came to me. Men who are condemned to die have a last meal the night before execution. Do they calm themselves with conversation with a friendly guard or chaplain? The seconds must leak away like water from the canteen of a desert traveler. The condemned face the future as the minutes slip away. But the fact is, all of us are waiting in a day-by-day and lifelong vigil for the summons.

With such happy thoughts, I must have drifted into sleep in spite of the pain, for the next thing I was conscious of was the chill of dew on my face and clothes. I wrapped the sleeping bag around me. In the gray light before dawn, spruce trees became visible. In panic I'd crawled above the hardwood zone into the balsams. Every tree looked like a Christmas tree. The pain in my left leg returned, and my hands and knees were raw from creeping.

Raising to look through the limbs, I spotted the creek far below, the small muddy lake and the gash in the mountainside where the slide had ripped away much of the slope. The tent was nowhere to be seen, buried under water. As the sun flared into view and touched the ridges with fire, it created quite a scene, though I was in no condition to enjoy the splendors of nature. Below I'd been miles from the nearest trail, and even further from the nearest road. But I'd been by a stream, and a stream will always lead you toward people. It was a long way to the creek.

While in recovery I'd found that pain can be lessened by thinking of something that interests you. It could be anything, a new car, a pretty woman, a place you want to visit, an anecdote that feeds your vanity, or a friend who has done you a favor. Such concentration won't erase your pain, but can serve as a temporary distraction. I looked below at the way I'd have to travel on my knees and belly. Survival itself would be the best opiate.

I won't bore you with details about how I pulled myself down the mountain, out of the spruces into the hardwoods, to get to the creek and follow the creek to lower elevations. I was scratched by spruce needles and briars, but at least I could see to avoid some of the sharper things. My hands were so badly cut from the night before that I hauled myself on elbows, the way they teach you in basic training to worm forward while holding your rifle. Soon my elbows were almost as raw as my hands.

When I was a teenager my friends and I had a little saying, if things went wrong or we needed cheering up. Later I repeated it to myself when depressed or stressed, just a few silly words: "You've got it made, in the shade, with lemonade, stirred with a spade," a nonsense rhyme, but catchy. I repeated it while working my way down the slope, and maybe it even helped some.

By the time I reached the creek, downstream from the landslide, I was worn out and aching. My knees throbbed, and my elbows, hands shredded. The broken shin bone didn't hurt as much, and I wondered if it was numbed by infection, or gangrene. In Hemingway's story "The Snows of Kilimanjaro" the protagonist grows delirious with gangrene and smells the stench of his own leg. Surely it was too early for gangrene to set in. That will come in good time, I told myself, when you're out of your head.

Even with the pain, I was thirsty. Maybe the pain

made the thirst worse. My mouth was cottony and my lips so parched they were splitting.

About halfway down the slope I found I could drag the sleeping bag no further. I was simply too weak to pull it, and sometimes my knees pinned the bag even as my hand tried to jerk it forward. I stopped to rest. Without the bag I'd have nothing to keep me warm at night but the windbreaker. There was a string at the head of the bag. With some maneuvering I laid the bag over my back and tied it at my neck, as a kind of cape.

I wrestled another hundred feet, but the bag caught on limbs and kept falling. Was there some way to use the bag to cushion my knees and hands? With my knife I could cut pieces of the bag, but how could they be attached? Reluctantly I dropped the bag aside. As I approached the stream, rocks bruised my elbows and knees. I ground my jaws and scrambled through jagged stones to the water, only to find the creek bed empty. The landslide had caught the water, and until the pond or lake overflowed, the creek was just pools warming among rocks. I lowered my face into one of the puddles and drank, then stopped, for if I swilled too fast I'd throw it up.

Easy does it, old boy, I said. Easy does it. I held my head up to give my stomach time to settle before gulping more. With head raised I heard voices. Hallucination? It was too good to believe that people were hiking this far up the valley. I crawled out of the creek bed and pushed myself up and tried to holler. But before a syllable gagged out of my throat, two men with rifles slung over their shoulders stepped into view, pushing a kind of stretcher rolling on a single bicycle wheel. The men had big bellies and red caps. I tried to yell, but was too weak to make more than a kind of squawk.

"Hep," I coughed out.

The men jerked in my direction, but couldn't let go of the stretcher because a large boar was strapped on it. Slowly they turned the vehicle over and laid it down and unslung their rifles. Pointing the barrels ahead they eased toward me. "Here," I said, knowing how strange I appeared on all fours, face scratched and swollen by bug bites.

"Who the hell are you?" one said, and aimed a high-powered rifle at my head.

I begged them to help me, told my story and apologized for being in such a wretched state. I knew they were poaching, had killed the boar out of season.

"Mister, we can't help you," one said.

"You never even seen us," the other added.

I assured them I would never report them. I just needed to get back to the highway, to a doctor. Their secret was safe with me.

"If you was to tattle you'd be sorry," the first one said and held the rifle to my head.

"We can't be no help," the other said. He seemed a little friendlier than his partner.

"Who are you?" the first one said. He had tobacco stains in the corners of his mouth. I told them I grew up in the mountains, but was a professor of geology at a college in the Piedmont. Even as I said it I saw that was the wrong tack to take.

"You're one of them professors?" the first man said.

"I need to get to the highway," I repeated, and showed them my wallet, which the second one grabbed.

They didn't say any more. One reached into his pocket and pulled out three slim plastic strings and threw them in front of me. They slung the rifles over their shoulders and with effort raised the wheeled device and headed down the valley. "Would you tell someone I'm here?" I called, but they didn't respond or look back.

When the poachers were out of sight I looked at the objects on the ground. They were ropes of beef jerky wrapped in plastic, the kind you get at convenience stores and bars. I ripped the cover off one and put the end in my mouth. It was salty and greasy, and tasted wonderful, but too tough to eat fast. I chewed and sucked the juice out of the meat, and placed the other two inside my shirt. I hated the men for leaving me, but was grateful they hadn't killed me. They would never tell anyone they'd seen me.

Heaving onto elbows, I followed their track with sweaty effort. The hunters stayed away from the creek to avoid rocks. But I couldn't stray far from the creek bed, for the jerky would make me even thirstier.

Looking at my watch, I figured I could go about two hundred yards in an hour, maybe a little more. At that rate, if lucky, I might crawl a mile before dark. It would take five days to reach the trail. The jerky would have to last me.

What you see from dirt-level is different from what you see when walking. I'd discovered that the world looks changed from a wheelchair. But on my belly and elbows things appeared even more altered. As I huffed and puffed and hauled myself, I noticed textures of soil, the sand and clay, roots of grass and bushes, grit and humus, the skeletons of rotting leaves, woolly worms, tiny flowers like bluets, sand sculped by runoff. Squirrels and rabbits watched me. Toads jumped out of my way. A possum stared at me, and I passed a yellow moccasin flower, creamy mallow blossoms, and several different kinds of ferns.

Once when I paused, hoping the pain in my left leg would subside, I noticed the edge of something circular in the dirt beside a rock. Scratching it loose, I found a copper or brass coin the size of a small medallion. Rubbing it clean exposed tiny markings, but no image. It was not unknown to find Spanish coins in the mountains, for the Spanish had come here in the sixteenth century looking for gold, enslaving Cherokees. But when I examined the coin in the sun, its marks appeared to be not in any alphabet I recognized, but a beautiful script of flourishes and curls, dots and knots, reminding me of Turkish. How strange to find a Turkish coin in the mountains of North Carolina. And then I remembered one explanation for the presence of Melungeon people in the mountains was that at the battle of Lepanto in 1571 the Spanish had taken so many Ottoman prisoners they dumped them on the coast of the Gulf of Mexico. The captives wandered inland and intermarried with Indians and later with escaped African slaves. One must have had a Turkish coin which he used for trade with indigenous people or for decoration.

As far as I knew, no one had ever found a Turkish coin in the mountains. My discovery would be of some importance. Flat on my belly and in pain, I'd done something significant, if I survived to report it.

Elbow-working along, as steady as possible, and re-lieved to have encountered no rattlesnakes, I may have achieved a mile by dark. With no sleeping bag, no grub but the Slim Jim jerky, I stopped by a small branch. At least there would be clean water. And I had my light windbreaker for the cool night. Flat on my back I must have quickly floated into sleep.

Waking, it was the soreness in my hands and knees and lower legs noticed first. But something had disturbed me. I listened, and heard a bird I didn't recognize off to the right. There was dew on my face and hair and on the jacket, cold enough to make me shiver. The woods were dim, shadowy, but charged with mystery and expectation. There is a time just before dawn when the woods wait for a signal for day to begin; air has an immanence.

A growl on my left, and a sound of breathing and scratching in the leaves. The dawn breeze came from that direction, so whatever it was, bear or panther, raccoon, had not smelled me. I tried to rise to look in that direction without making any noise. Luckily the damp leaves didn't rustle. At first I saw nothing. All was shadows under the brush. I tried to recall how the trees nearby had looked the day before.

There was another grunt, and shaking limbs. I stared into the shadows to adjust my sight. Then I recalled you see better in the dark from the corners of your eyes.

Turning sideways, I found a form materializing in the gray light. At almost the same instant I saw the bear, he smelled or recognized me. Neither of us moved.

What advice was there was for confronting a bear? At least this was a black bear and not a grizzly. Black bears are supposed to run, unless you get between them and their foraging, or their cubs. But I was not standing up like a human. I couldn't rise, not even to the height of a bear. Bears would eat anything, even human flesh, I feared, if it was available. Could the bear smell the blood of my cuts and sores? Should I move and shout, or be still?

Like everyone else, I'd thought of my death from time to time. Would I die of cancer in a hospital, or suddenly in a car crash? Would I have a heart attack while hiking far back in the mountains? Maybe being eaten by a bear was not the worst fate, to return to the wilderness as a meal for a burly beast.

The smell of a bear is hard to describe, like a closet of dirty clothes, of rancid unwashed hair. He could probably smell my sweat-crusted skin and bloody sores. As my eyes adjusted and the woods grew lighter, I saw the bear was no more than forty feet away, able to pounce on me in seconds. If I yelled defiantly, would it scare him? If I waved my arms would he back away?

Even as we stared at each other, I knew this was a defining moment. For a hundred thousand years my ancestors had confronted bears and wolves, boars and panthers, woolly mammoths, saber-toothed tigers, maybe lions, buffalos and rhinos in the wild. Some were eaten, and some survived by stealth, luck, or skill. Would I be the last in the ancient chain of confrontation? Would I prove myself worthy in the moment of testing? These thoughts seethed through my head, but the fact was, I was frozen by surprise and fear. The bear was probably just as surprised as me as he foraged for a snack before dawn.

Our standoff probably lasted only a few seconds,

but it seemed hours, years, echoing down corridors of centuries and the rise of civilization. I was on trial with all my forebears, and the bear was a judge in his black robes. My mettle was measured, and I was found wanting. My only excuse was my handicap and wounds.

And then it was over. In the gray light, as I saw him clearly, the bear grunted with contempt and turned away, to show he had no fear and could not be routed. Leaving a turd and his smell in the air to mark his authority, he slouched away until lost in the brush. I gasped, for I'd been holding my breath, so starved for oxygen I was a little dizzy, and trembling.

It took a while to calm myself. I was lucky, for the bear had not attacked me in my weakened state. But I was still miles from the trail, and further from the highway. I'd lost my cell phone in the panic after the avalanche. I still had a pocket knife, but the good old boys had taken my wallet. Two Slim Jims were still inside my shirt. Breathing deep and regular, I tore open one of the covers and began to chew the salty cord.

Through trees, the ridges on both sides of the valley were visible, burnished with sunrise. The valley remained in shadow, but the peaks were on fire. In my first geology class in college I'd been taught the Blue Ridge mountains were the oldest on the continent, older than the Alleghenies or the Rockies, older than the Sierra. The Alleghenies and Cumberlands rose mostly in long running ridges as the earth buckled and folded under the stress of tectonics. But the Blue Ridge had boiled up between plates, in turmoil, with turbulent forces, where shapes were irregular, some long, some tumbled, as though churned and left with scrambled features, each ridge one-of-a-kind, defying patterns or overall arrangement. Every valley and watershed looked odd, the terrain unpredictable in its disposition.

It seemed apropos that I was lost in such a crazy quilt of mountains, in a crazy pattern of bad luck, with a tiny bit of good luck. At least the bear hadn't slapped

me down and eaten me. I might live to see my wife
and children and grandchildren, if I could writhe and
wrestle a few more miles over rough terrain.

According to my watch, I'd spent half an hour
chewing the jerky, pausing once to lean over the branch
and drink where a muscle of water curved over rock.
There was just enough in the salty meat to make me
hungrier still, but I dared not consume the last one.

You better get on with it, old boy, I exhorted myself.
If I wanted to live I must reach a doctor before infection
claimed the broken leg. If I couldn't crawl and no one
found me, nature would take its course. My flesh would
feed the buzzards and other animals. My skeleton might
be found sometime, far in the mountains. And I would
return to the soil with no coffin or embalming. I raised
my head and began to elbow-walk forward.

Avoiding the rocky creekbank, I must have made a
third of a mile by noon. Toads and terrapins got out of my
way, and a copperhead whisked off in the leaves. A skunk
appeared, and I kept still until it foraged away into the
undergrowth. And then I saw a paper bag ahead, sitting
upright and looking crisp. Drawing closer I recognized it
was from McDonald's, and appeared to be full. Was it
bugged, a booby trap, the kind you see in movies?

But I couldn't restrain myself and looked into the
bag, found a Big Mac and a large packet of fries, and
in the bottom a crusty fried apple pie. My next thought
was: had someone hiking or fishing left it there for their
lunch and planned to return? Maybe they anticipated a
picnic. For two days I'd eaten nothing but the strings of
jerky. My belly was sore from scraping the ground and
my shirt in tatters. The contents of the bag were cold,
but still had the aroma of hamburger meat and fries.

Could somebody be watching me to see what I did?
Had Lois sent someone to search for me when I didn't
answer the cell phone? Not knowing exactly where I
was, had they left the bag there for me to find? Lois
was the kindest person I'd ever known. She was kind

to everyone. In my recovery I learned again what I had known all along, that with Lois I was the luckiest man alive. When I hadn't been found, she'd placed meals in places in the wilderness where I might find them.

But I also knew that could not be true, for Lois would never choose fast food. She would place wholesome granola bars, or a salad, fruit, nuts, oranges, bananas to be discovered. This must be the stash of someone planning to return. Still puzzled, I found myself chewing French fries. There was no decision. I was too famished to make decisions, just crammed the cold fries in my mouth, to gulp them down, then caught myself, and chewed slower, to avoid throwing up. If someone returned for their feast I would explain my predicament.

There were napkins in the bag and I wiped my hands before attacking the big burger. The dressing in the sandwich streamed out when the bun was squeezed, and covered my hands and wrists, but I didn't care. The bread and meat tasted too good to be explained. I relished every bit down to the last crumb. My sticky hands would have to be washed in the nearest branch. I saved the fried pie for later. Who knew when I'd find another order from McDonald's?

It came to me that the two boar poachers had left the bag. Who else knew where I was, or the shape I was in? They'd threatened to kill me if I reported them. They knew I had nothing to eat but the Slim Jims, or toads or whatever I could catch with my hands. The bag must have been a bribe for my silence, a favor they hoped I'd remember, if I survived, which was not a foregone conclusion.

Whoever had left the junk food, I was grateful. As I was contemplating the good fortune in the context of my bad luck, a motor noise seeped over the ridge. While it grew louder I struggled to turn in that direction, as a helicopter floated above the peak. The rotors and the engine made a harsh thud-thud-thud that echoed off the ridges. As it drew nearer, I had to signal it somehow.

Grabbing the white bag, I held it high as I could reach
and wagged it back and forth. A gust not noticed before
grabbed the bag and flung it away into the brush.

"Help!" I screamed and waved, and fell onto my
hands. When I raised again the chopper was far away to
the south. I was as crushed as some member of a cargo
cult in New Guinea, begging for gifts from the sky that
never came. The sky was empty, but at least my belly
was full. I lay down to rest before moving again.

When I woke, the sky had clouded over, and the air
smelled of rain. That was one challenge not considered
before: what would I do in a storm in my present state?
I'd need a tree to shelter under, preferably an evergreen,
a spruce. But I'd left the balsams and crawled down
among hardwoods. On my knees I looked around for
the closest pines. If there was lightning I should avoid an
isolated tree. To my left I spotted some hemlocks, about
two hundred yards away, probably along a branch.

With the pie in my left hand and using elbows and
knees, I worked in that direction, banging bones on
rocks, face stung by twigs. If I got soaked, with night
coming on, I could contract pneumonia in my sorry
condition. I had no way to start a fire. The air tasted
of storm. Once I paused and heard rain advancing up
the valley, like an army marching on tiny feet, racing,
closing in. I hurried, with the line of hemlocks in view.

The first drops hit my neck just as I rolled under
the lower limbs of a hemlock. And then the torrent,
loud as a waterfall, dumped on the trees. I couldn't
stay dry under the hemlocks, but was spared the worst
lash of the elements. It was a while before the limbs
above started to drip. To calm myself, I ate the fried pie,
slowly, savoring every crumb. Comfort food indeed.

That night, as I hunkered under the limbs, the
hamburger and fries and pie in my belly worked as
fuel to keep me warm. The windbreaker grew wet
and also my jeans. I tried to think myself warm, using
thought as fuel. As a boy I'd tried that, when caught in

a thunderstorm far from the house. And I also had pain to warm me. Pain is heat. I burned thoughts to ward off a cold and pneumonia, using what adrenaline was left like oil in a stove or lamp.

To keep alert, I told stories and recited poems learned in childhood, "The Raven," "I Wandered Lonely as a Cloud," "Thanatopsis." I remembered the story of Davy Crockett, alone and soaked in the woods, climbing up and down a tree all night to stay warm. I recited over and over the requiem Robert Louis Stevenson wrote for himself, especially the last four lines:

And this be the verse you grave for me:
Here he lies where he longed to be;
Home is the sailor, home from the sea,
And the hunter home from the hill.

I quoted other poems too, but the Stevenson epitaph was the one I kept repeating.

When I was in the hospital recovering from brain surgery, I realized I'd come close to death, and at my age was close to death anyway. Death was no longer a stranger, nor a friend. Death was only a milestone, a fact, deserving neither terror nor fancy words uttered at funerals. Stevenson had it right. What I had thought of as a children's poem contained wisdom.

I slept a little toward dawn, as the rain slacked. It was the kind of sleep where you don't know you're asleep, as your thoughts blend into a dream. And with surprise you recognize you've been dreaming.

My clothes were damp, my feet cold. My socks had worn away the first day as I groveled over the ground. My feet were scratched and sore, and my supplies consisted of one Slim Jim and a knife in my left pocket. I felt to see if it was still there. And then I touched the right pocket, and found a cylinder the size of a shotgun shell. It was my waterproof canister of matches. In the panic of landslide and rising water I'd forgotten it. One half fitted over the other. Inside were maybe six kitchen matches placed there for emergencies. It seemed

impossible the container was still in my pocket and that
I'd forgotten it. The matches were dry. I closed the case
and hauled myself out of the trees as sun illuminated
the wet and dripping valley.

Finding the matches was a miraculous surprise,
but without dry fuel they were useless. Everything,
including sticks and leaves and grass, was waterlogged.
Daniel Boone would have had tinder and flint and steel
in a waterproof box to spark a fire. I had no tinder,
and little experience at starting fires in a dripping forest.
Think, I whispered to myself. A fire may be your only
hope. What would Davy Crockett do?

I won't waste your time telling you all the things I
considered, finding dry grass under a grape vine, looking
for dry limbs under a rock. Finally, I remembered that if
dead limbs near the base of a white pine could be split,
dry, resinous wood would be exposed in their core.
There was a white pine close to the creek and I crawled
in that direction.

It took about half an hour to reach the pine. Dead
limbs near the ground were soaked on the outside.
It took some effort to break several, so brittle they
hummed and stung my hand when snapped. There was
only one knot of any size. I dragged the limbs two at
a time into an open space covered by grass and weeds.
The vegetation was heavy with wetness.

It took another half hour to clear a hearth three or
four feet in diameter. I might have only one chance to
start a fire to warm myself. Within the bare yard on the
wet ground I began to shave a pine knot. The wood was
bright as hard candy, toffee candy. I carved the knot
into a hundred shavings, then split one of the limbs and
shaved off splinters from the heart wood, and added
them to the heap. I piled the sticks at the edge of my
little clearing.

Trembling with fear and weakness, I coughed and
sneezed. Hovering over my stack of curls and splinters,
I struck one of the precious matches, but it broke and

the head flew off into the weeds. I tried another, but the flame flared and went out. Don't let this be like one of those adventure films where nothing works until the very last possible chance, I prayed.

With care I struck a third match and placed the head among the curls and splinters. One piece began to smoke, and a flame caught on the edge. A splinter caught, and then another, and they burst into flame. And then the separate flames coalesced into a larger fire. I added the other split limbs to the conflagration.

As the fire reached knee-high, my work had only begun. I flung myself over briars to the nearest oak tree and gathered sticks and dead limbs. It took many trips before I had the flames roaring up five or six feet, far above my head. I warmed myself in the light from the bonfire, turning my left side and then the right.

As I basked in the heat, the sound of an airplane echoed over the mountains. If it came my way surely it would see the smoke. With my jacket I might make smoke signals, but the fire was too hot and too high for that. I'd just burn my jacket and achieve nothing. As the plane slipped into view, I saw it was a twin-engine Beechcraft, maybe a mile high. Unable to stand, I could only wave my arms, then fall back on my belly. I yelled, but knew that was silly. I threw on more wet limbs to make smoke, but the plane was soon out of sight and sound.

Where was the helicopter of the State Police looking for marijuana patches in the mountains?

I stayed by the fire until my clothes dried and the last of the sticks had burned down to coals. I could have gathered more sticks to rebuild the fire, but what was the point? The thing was to get my ass on the way.

I was about three, maybe four miles from the trail. Grinding teeth against the ache in elbows and knees, I forced myself ahead, as sun warmed the ground and cicadas called for mates in the trees. The only way to deal with the pain was to concentrate on work, on my goal.

The harder the work, the less important the pain. You've got it made in the shade, but there was no lemonade.

I hadn't gone more than a furlong when something stabbed me on the neck, and then on the left arm. A buzzing told me I'd crawled close to a yellowjacket nest. They build their homes in the ground, under a rock or root. I hadn't spotted the hole into the nest, but the air was swarming with black and yellow warriors. No use to swat at them. I crawled frantically away as they stung my cheeks and ears.

When the jackets finally abandoned me, I was only a hundred yards beyond the hole. The stings throbbed on my face and arms, and the poison raced in my blood. As far as I knew I wasn't allergic to stings, but the pain of the venom made the pain in my hands and legs less severe.

I rolled on my back to feel the swellings on my face, then heard a dog, a hound, baying. A black and tan came sniffing and yelping out of the trees. There was a man behind the dog in a gray uniform, and then another. I rolled onto my belly to see them better. The first man had a pistol on his hip and the second carried a rifle. I'd never been happier to see other human beings.

"Hell!" I called, my mouth too dry to speak. The dog trotted close and sniffed and whimpered. The men followed and stopped in front of me.

"Thank you so much," I coughed out. "I couldn't have made it much further." I gasped how happy I was to see them, and how grateful I was they'd come looking for me. I asked if Lois had alerted them to my location. I wouldn't tell them about the poachers.

"What is your full name?" the first man said.

I told him, and could hardly breathe with relief and exhilaration, gratitude, and embarrassment. I would explain to them all that had happened.

"Mister, I'm arresting you for killing a boar out of season, and hunting without a license," the first man said and read me my rights.

"You're arresting me?"

"You have the right to remain silent," he said.

As he spoke I soon realized what had happened. The two poachers had been arrested and claimed that I was the real poacher. I'd killed the boar and they had subdued me, and brought in the evidence, like good, law-abiding citizens. They told the game warden and police where I was, and showed them my wallet, emptied of cash. They said I'd fought them and hurt myself, and they'd meant to report me.

I began laughing, and the two game wardens looked at me like I was berserk. "That's so wonderful," I said again and again. If I could have stood I would have kissed them both.

"I'll call in the helicopter," the older man said, resting his hand on the revolver in its holster.

HURRICANE

Quentin had tried to organize a union among the laborers and been fired. And because I supported him, I was fired too. We'd been building a road across the Everglades from the east side of Florida to the west coast. We were on the crew that chopped the right of way through swamp and jungle, snakes, alligators, mosquitoes, flies, leeches, and hornets, with a rawhiding boss-man. It was unbearable work, but it was also the depths of the Depression and thousands of men were willing to work cheap and keep their mouths shut. The boss had called the sheriff to run us off the site, and a deputy sheriff in overalls named Brisendine said we had an hour to get out of the county or he'd lock us up. They would tolerate no outside agitators in Dade. He had a cage of hounds on the back of his truck, and warned if we tried to hide in the woods he'd track us down.

It was early afternoon when we started out, and we hadn't had any dinner. The clerk had given us our pay and told us to get on our way. I wasn't hungry yet. I was too surprised and excited by all that had happened to think of eating. But I'd be hungry later on. When you're seventeen you don't want to miss many meals. The hollow place in my belly would soon start to grow tight and sore.

It was farther back to the highway than I remembered. I'd walked to the camp two weeks before, but had forgotten the long road in the heat. The white seashell track ahead seemed to wobble and flop around and gobble up our steps. A black snake bright as patent leather stretched across the road in front of us. Quentin picked it up by the tail and flung it into the swamp.

"We could go south," Quentin said. "We could go down to the Keys."

I asked what kind of work we could find there.

"We could live on the beach and catch fish."

I asked how we would catch fish with no hooks or lines or nets.

"There's got to be tackle shops on the Keys."

Finally, we heard traffic in the distance and knew the highway couldn't be too much farther. Trucks droned and snorted, and gargled as they geared down or up. The sun hammered on my back and on my head.

"We could go to Miami and look for work," Quentin said.

"Don't you want to head north where it's cooler? We could go to the mountains and live on fresh corn." I thought of the cool spring at home and the bowls Mama would put on the table for dinner, cornbread and beans, and new potatoes, hot coffee and cold buttermilk. And sometimes she'd make a peach cobbler or, better still, a blackberry cobbler, for dinner.

"I don't want to go anywhere there's a coal mine," Quentin said.

A car crunched up behind us and we stepped to the side of the road. It was the sheriff's car, slowing as it passed, and one of the deputies who'd threatened us gave us a hard look. Dust boiled up behind the vehicle and we turned away and put hands over our noses while the dust settled.

As the air cleared, I noticed a Model A pickup following the sheriff's car. Brisendine's hounds were loaded in a cage in the back and when the dogs spotted Quentin and me they started bellowing. I thought at first the truck was slowing so it wouldn't raise more dust, but it rolled to a stop and the driver got out. Brisendine carried a chain and he had a pistol strapped to his waist. Tobacco juice stained the corners of his mouth. I kept walking and Quentin followed.

"Hey!" Brisendine yelled. "You think you can spit on the law in Dade County and go free? We don't take kindly to outside agitators." I stopped to answer him.

The deputy took the pistol from the holster and held it in his right hand and the chain in the left. He stepped closer, but I turned again and started walking. A shot kicked up dust in front of me. The hounds raised a louder howl.

Brisendine held the gun on me and Quentin. The sheriff's car was now out of sight. I guessed it had already reached the highway, headed toward Miami, and the long white road back to the camp was empty. There was nobody to see what the deputy in overalls did, except his dogs. He could turn the dogs loose to chase us, or he could shoot us and roll our bodies into the swamp and nobody would ever know the difference. Mama and Papa didn't know where I was and Quentin's folks probably didn't know where he was either.

Brisendine rattled the chain and stepped closer. "You think you can piss on the law and go free?" he said. "You think folks in Florida got no law?"

He aimed the pistol at me and stepped closer, shaking the chain like he was daring me to grab for it. "I'm going to hurt you," he said. "You boys need a lesson to remember."

Quentin was farther away from Brisendine than me, and he started running toward the highway. The deputy raised the pistol toward Quentin, and then lowered it and turned to me again. "I'll do you first," he said.

If I started running Brisendine would shoot me. If he killed me he'd kick my body into the swamp and buzzards would pick my bones. But what he wanted most was to whip me with the chain, to beat me bloody and watch me hurt.

"My dogs need some justice," he said. "They've got religion and they need to see some law and order."

As I watched his little eyes, I thought how crazy it was for citizens of a county, in the name of law, to hire a man so cruel and vengeful to maintain peace and uphold the law. Brisendine was more dangerous than most criminals, and yet he wore a badge on his overalls. As long as he held the pistol he could shoot me any time.

He swung the chain like a whip or heavy lasso. If I lunged for the pistol he'd hit me with the chain. If I grabbed for the chain he'd shoot me or hit me over the head with the gun. He swung the chain and stung me on the knee, then jerked the length back before I could grab it. Even though the links just touched me it felt like I'd been hit by a bullet. I must have hollered out, for he said, "Don't feel so good to be hurt, does it?"

The pain in my leg was so bad I thought I was going to fall. He meant to kill me with the chain, or at least cripple me. All it would take would be a few more licks. I could throw myself over the bank and roll into the weeds and brush. But then he'd turn the dogs loose after me. Or I could try to rush him with my head down as he reached back to swing the chain again. But then he'd just shoot me in the belly. Or I could try grabbing the pistol while he was hitting me with the chain. None of the choices was good.

I decided that my only hope was to leap at Brisendine's chest, which he wouldn't expect. If he shot he might miss me, and if I was quick enough I might knock him down and take the gun. I was bracing to jump when Quentin stood up on the road's shoulder behind Brisendine. He'd run up the road a way and then crawled back out of sight, along the canal. The deputy caught the surprise on my face and turned to look just in time for a rock Quentin flung to hit him in the temple. Brisendine fell backwards in the road before me. I dropped on top of him and jerked the chain out of his hand. Quentin dashed across the road and grabbed the pistol.

The deputy lay still. I was going to hit him with the chain, but he was out cold. Blood trickled from the side of his head where the rock had struck. Quentin and I stood up and looked at the deputy. The dogs howled in the truck, but they were in the cage. They yelped and clawed the wire of the cage and climbed over each other.

Quentin said he used to kill rabbits with rocks in Kentucky. It was all he had to eat sometimes, when the mines closed.

We had to decide what to do with Brisendine. Quentin suggested we just leave him there and get away fast as we could. But I listened to the deputy's heart and found he was still breathing. He would come to soon and be after us. If we were walking and hitch-hiking he'd catch up with us before we got out of Dade County.

I told Quentin we had to put Brisendine in the truck with the dogs and tie him up and drive as far north as possible, before we left him beside the road or in a swamp. That might give us time to get out of the state of Florida. We looked in the truck and found some binder's twine and tied his hands and feet. And we toted the deputy to the truck and put him in the cage with the hounds. Then we climbed in the truck cab and I took the wheel.

"Do you have a driver's license?" Quentin said.

"No, but I drove Papa's Model A around the farm." I put the truck in gear and rumbled to the highway and turned north.

"I didn't want to hurt anybody," Quentin said. "One reason I had to leave the coal camp and Harlan was to get away from the beatings and killings between the union and company agents." Quentin said people had been murdered with machine guns and dynamite where he came from. He said the miners went on strike because they got paid so little, and because the mines were so dangerous. He said the company brought in outside workers called scabs. The camp where the scabs lived was dynamited and some strikers got killed by the Baldwin-Phelps agents.

"I had to get away before I was killed, or killed somebody myself."

Steering north alongside the drooping telegraph and telephone lines, I gritted my teeth to keep my anger intact. If I couldn't keep up my fury I didn't know what I'd do. Before we had only gotten ourselves fired. But now we were in much bigger trouble.

"You ain't been out in the world much," Quentin said. "You're not used to people's meanness."

I was stung by his words, accusing me of being just a kid.

"You were raised by decent people," Quentin said. "I can tell that."

To keep my anger strong, I wanted to argue with him, but to argue I'd have to say I didn't come from decent folks. I'd have to pretend my life on the little farm on Green River was rough as life in the coal camps.

"The deputy had it coming," I said. If I lost my anger it would be like admitting we had to give ourselves up and there was no hope for us. The police wouldn't forget that one of us had hit Brisendine, who was, after all, an officer of the law.

It was only a matter of time before the sheriff and other deputies would come looking for Brisendine and the Model A truck. They'd alert the highway patrol, who'd start searching for the truck and dogs.

"I figure it will take them about an hour to come back and look for him," I said and pointed to the cage in back.

"If you're wrong we'll end up in the pen, or dead."

A police car roared toward us but went on past. We drove through a little town with fruit stands and a hotdog diner and a gas station. The gas gauge showed there was less than an eighth of a tank left in the Model A. But if we stopped to get gas somebody would spot the deputy tied-up in the cage with the dogs. And the dogs' bellowing and yelping would attract attention.

"How are we going to get any gas?" I said.

"Stop outside the town and I'll walk back and buy a can of gas."

I kept on driving, past another filling station and a row of shacks. But there were more houses, and then a small depot by the railroad tracks. And after that we passed a tourist court.

Finally, we reached open country, where there was just water in a ditch on one side of the highway and telegraph poles and train tracks on the other. But I never found any place to pull off.

"You've got to stop," Quentin said. "It's already a mile back to a filling station."

"You want me to stop in the middle of the road?"

"It's already too far to walk."

I told him I'd turn around and go back. I'd stop across the road or down the street from one of the filling stations and maybe nobody would notice Brisendine in the cage with the dogs. But just then the hounds set up an even louder howl. They bellowed and whimpered, yelped and groaned like a snake or weasel had slipped into the cage.

"The dogs are going crazy," Quentin said.

And then we heard another voice, a man's voice, yelling, "Hey, stop this damned truck!" And the cage shook and something banged on the back of the cab. Brisendine had woke and was kicking the cage. Quentin and I looked at each other. Brisendine would be yelling at every passing car and person beside the road. He and the dogs were making such a fuss we'd be noticed for sure. We couldn't go through another town and we couldn't slow down.

I reckon the same thought went through our heads. We didn't have time to get gas. We had to drive off the highway and into the woods before anybody heard the deputy yelling.

"Help me!" Brisendine shouted at a passing car. "I'm an officer of the law!" he screamed as a truck went by. He yelled something about kidnapping and hanging, but I didn't catch most of it.

"Look for a side road," Quentin said.

"I hadn't thought of that," I said.

"No use to get snappy."

I had to hold onto my anger if I was to keep going. Anger was the only thing propping me up, keeping me together. Anger was the one thing that kept me from facing my own hopelessness. I'd stood up for Quentin, and he'd been fired for trying to help the work crew. And he'd saved me from the deputy who meant to kill me with the chain, or at least cripple me. It was silly to be short with Quentin, or to blame him. And yet he irritated me because I was scared, and he was right.

"Look out for a side road," I said.

"I'll think about it."

With the deep ditch to the left, we'd have to find a way across the railroad tracks on the right. And even if the road ran to a little town we'd have to take it.

"Maybe we can shut him up and dump him in the woods and go on," Quentin said.

"I'm not going to touch him again," I said. I thought if we didn't kill Brisendine or hurt him any more we might still be able to get out of the state of Florida. If the mean deputy was killed they'd look for us all over the country. But if we just gave him a ride in his own truck with his dogs and left him unharmed, somewhere in the woods, maybe the whole thing would blow over. Brisendine kicked the cage so hard it made the truck shake. The dogs howled and the Model A rocked and bounced. I steered steady on the right lane and looked for a side road.

"You will fry in the chair!" the deputy screamed.

Cars passed and drivers tried to get a good look at the cage in the bed. Another police car passed. It was only a matter of time until somebody stopped us to see what the yelling and commotion were about.

"You better think of something," Quentin said.

"I'm driving," I said, meaning I was too busy to think. And then I spotted a sign ahead: "Drum 4 Miles." An arrow pointed to the right. I didn't know how far it was to the beach, but figured the town of Drum must be close to the ocean. Soon as we reached the little road I turned and banged across the tracks. The dogs whimpered and bayed.

"Let me out and you can take the truck!" Brisendine yelled.

I drove on down the road made of crushed seashells and sand, much like the road into the Everglades. Palmettoes and brush lined the ruts. Vines along the shoulders had crawled into the routes and been mashed by tires.

"There!" Quentin shouted, pointing to a shadow of track going out into the thicket. It might have been a wagon trail or a logging trail. Limbs reached almost over the trace. I turned into the narrow way and branches lashed the sides of the cab. I could barely see the path ahead, but drove slowly. A pole had fallen across the ruts and I bumped the Model A over it.

"Stop!" Brisendine yelled. I reckon he thought we would take him into the woods to kill him. I saw a place where there'd been a campfire, and stopped the truck beside the scattered charcoal. Bottles and cans lay in weeds. I left the key in the switch and got out. The dogs made a terrible racket, and the deputy yelled, "Let me a-loose and I won't tell on you!"

Quentin took the pistol from the cab, but I told him to put it back, leave it with the chain. "We might need it," he said. I explained that if we took the pistol they'd say we were armed and dangerous, and could be shot on sight. If we just left it there they might give up on us once we got out of the county, and out of the state.

"Untie me!" Brisendine hollered. "I'll give you my money." Soon as we got away he could untie his hands with his teeth and reach through the bars of the cage and find we hadn't locked the padlock. He could let himself out easily.

Quentin and I started walking in the sand back to the road. "Let's get to the highway," I said, loud, so Brisendine could hear. But the dogs made such a fuss I doubt he did catch my words.

"If we get on the highway they'll arrest our asses for sure," Quentin said.

"That's why we're turning toward the beach," I whispered. When we got to the little road we turned left toward the town of Drum. The road ran between thickets till we reached a kind of river. A wooden bridge spanned the water, but the river didn't seem to be moving, and the water smelled marshy.

"Where does this river come from?" I said.

"Must be a tidal creek." Quentin said the water rose in this kind of stream when the tide came in, and went down again when the tide washed out. I'd forgotten about tides. In the mountains a tide means a flash flood. I could smell salt in the air. The bridge was rickety and sloped down and sideways.

Beyond the bridge the road ran between reeds and tall grass, pools of water wrinkled by wind, and mounds and ridges of sandy dirt. We passed a house standing six or seven feet high on poles. An old Black woman was taking clothes off a line in the backyard. The clothes flapped in the breeze.

The town was just a row of houses along a sandy street. There was a little church and what looked like a boarding house with porches all around. There didn't seem to be anybody about. A dog growled at us, then slunk away between houses. A store stood on the corner where another little street crossed the main street. I told

Quentin we'd have to stop and buy something to eat, something to carry with us, things that would keep, in cans and jars.

I looked past the store and across the street where a boat rested on its side and birds circled, yakking. Beyond a kind of ridge rose in a gray-blue sheet as far as you could see. I thought at first it was some kind of grass or gray sand heaped up in a slope.

"What is that?" I said.

"That's the ocean."

I felt silly. I'd known we were close to the ocean, but somehow it didn't look like what I'd expected. I'd thought the ocean would be flat, but this thing rose up out of the sand and bulged against the sky far out until it disappeared in mist. I wondered why the ocean seemed to climb away from us. I thought of the term "high seas."

And closer in, waves swept in long white lines that stretched out in foaming tongues across the sand. Wave followed wave in repeating gestures across wet beach, and crumbled into froth.

"That's the ocean?" I said.

"You sound disappointed."

I stood and watched the waves unfold and roll across the almost level sand. They seemed to fall from the height of the ocean and crash and spread out in glittering pieces of foam. The ocean was alive, with a beating heart or pulse that stretched itself and shivered in the breeze. Arms of spray reached out here and there. I wished I had a pencil to draw the scene.

"It's better if only one of us goes into the store," Quentin said. "That way if the police come asking about two boys they'll be thrown off."

I volunteered to go into the store. Quentin gave me five dollars and said he'd walk on up the beach and I could catch up with him. "Don't take my five dollars and head south," he said.

"Don't you keep walking so far I can't catch up," I said, and hit him on the shoulder, but pulled the punch.

The store reminded me of the little stores back home. There was the drink cooler and a glass case with candy bars. Shelves of canned goods lined the walls. But instead of hoes and shovels and harness and seeds and other farm tools, there was fishing tackle for sale. A big stuffed fish stretched on the wall. I got several cans of sardines and Vienna sausage. And I picked some cans of pork and beans, some cheese, and a can of salmon.

"Going camping?" the man behind the counter said.

"Thought I'd head south and do some fishing," I said.

"There's weather on the way," the clerk said.

I bought two spools of fishing line, some sinkers and hooks, and a section of leader.

"Trout ain't running in the creeks right now," the man said. "But you might catch a sheep-head." He looked sour and uninterested, which suited me. I didn't want him to ask more questions.

"I'm headed south anyway."

"Better fishing north of here."

I carried the bag outside and walked across the beach almost to where the waves came licking over the sand, and then turned north. It was surprising how hard the sand was where waves had washed up. It felt like the sand had been glued stiff by the water. A wave swept in like a wing over the sand and then seethed away. It was getting late in the afternoon and I could feel the damp salt on my face.

I must have gone a mile before I spotted Quentin, sitting back from the beach just under a dune. The sun was low in the tall grass behind him. He'd taken off his shoes and rolled up his pants. He said it would be dark soon and we'd better find a place to camp out of sight. "The cops can drive along the beach," he said. "And the Coast Guard patrols the beach too."

We must have walked two more miles along the surf before getting out of sight of the town of Drum. Then we turned left toward the sunset and climbed over dunes until we found a hollow place between two ridges of sand. I reckon water had stood in the hollow, but had dried up. Pieces of driftwood littered the floor.

"Did you get any matches?" Quentin said. I slapped the bag like I was feeling for matches, but hadn't bought any.

"Good thing I have some," Quentin said and laughed.

We gathered dry grass and sticks and pieces of driftwood and started a fire on the bottom of the trough, out of the breeze. The driftwood burned different colors, the way fruitwood will. Quentin said it was salt in the wood that made so many colors. The blaze flared up with purples and greens and pinks, just as it got dark, though the sky in the west was still red and gold. Quentin looked through the stuff in the bag and took out the fishing line and box of hooks. The sardine cans and the Vienna cans had keys to roll back the lids, but the other cans would have to be cut open. Quentin took out his pocket knife and jabbed the point into the top of a can of pork and beans.

"Have you used that to clean your toenails?" I said.

"Yeah, but I wiped the blade off."

We heated two cans of pork and beans and ate beans and sardines and Viennas and soda crackers, and watched the colorful flames dance. The stars had come out and sparks from the fire seemed to fly up and wink among the stars. The sand was soft as a cushioned couch.

"You know what else we haven't got?" Quentin said as he finished the sardines and tossed the can into the fire.

"Something to drink," I said.

"Damn right." He said we'd be OK until morning, but we'd get awful thirsty. He said we could live a week without food, but wouldn't survive more than a day or two without water. Now that he'd mentioned it, I started to feel dry. I was full of soda crackers and sardines and pork and beans. But I thought of water from the cool spring at home. I thought of water running out of a spigot, and the way water twists and warps as it comes from a faucet. I remembered the way clear water splashes and catches sunlight, and the way water spins as it goes down a drain. I finished the last juice from a can of pork and beans.

The fire crackled and the stars seemed to come closer. A breeze yawned over the dunes and whipped the flames. The sand was soft as a hammock under me.

"This sure beats the coal mine," Quentin said.

"And the cornfield."

I wondered if Brisendine was still in the cage with the dogs. I wondered if they were looking for us along the highway. "Tomorrow we'll fish," Quentin said and took out his harmonica and blew it a little, but I was already too sleepy to listen.

I'd never thought about how hard it would be to find drinking water near the ocean. That night I slept on the sand with the roar of the waves in my ears and dreamed of drinking from the pump at home. I dreamed of scooping up water with both hands and splashing my face, and licking cold drops off my lips. Later in the dream Quentin and I climbed over dunes until we found a deep hollow where we dug with our hands till we found a pool of water. I bent down to drink, but the liquid tasted like the dust of cement.

I must have been awfully tired, for I slept until the sun was up, coming over the dunes and sparkling off the ocean. I felt like I'd been rocked to sleep by the dunes, rocked in a cradle all night. I was rested and strengthened, but thirsty. My leg where Brisendine had hit me with the chain was sore. But my thirst was worse than the soreness. "We've got to find a spring," I said.

"Or a house with a well."

It hadn't occurred to me that a house near the beach would have a well. But soon as Quentin said it, I saw that every house had to have water, and there must be fresh water underground, even beside the ocean. As we ate more beans I noticed something different about the weather, but couldn't say how it was different. The sun rose through clouds in pink and gold glory. The sky was partly clear and the breeze mild as it had been the night before. But something in the air was new, like the air pressure had changed, or something else had altered. I asked Quentin if the air felt changed to him.

"Feels like it might rain."

We packed our stuff in the paper bag, buried the empty cans, and started walking up the beach again. The tide was far out and the beach was a wide, glistening highway. We strolled along the damp sand because it was firm and smooth. Birds whirled and swooped and strutted on the wet sea front.

"We've got to find a spring," I said.

"We'll come to a house if we keep walking."

I was going to ask Quentin why he was so sure, and then I spotted a roof far up the coast. It was so distant I couldn't tell what kind of building it was. Quentin saw the roof and pointed. "See," he said, "I told you."

Wind picked up and held steady as we walked toward the house. The wind swung around, not from the ocean, but from the south. The air seemed to push us along as we crossed the stretches of beach. Little by little the house grew bigger. My lips were dry and my mouth felt like dry flannel.

"I hope somebody's at the house," I said.

"Don't matter, we'll pump water from the well."

As we came closer I saw the house had two stories and a wide porch, sitting back from the ocean on a kind of rise. There was a smaller building beside it and another building out back. It was the kind of house with dormer windows like you might see on a street. But as we got nearer I noticed something was wrong with the windows. Instead of shiny panes of glass there were just boards.

Quentin said the owners must use it only in the winter and nailed planks over the windows and doors to keep it safe. We climbed across the dune and found tire tracks in the sand beside the house, and shoe prints around the porch. Somebody had been there that morning.

At the back of the house a wide porch was screened in. The door was nailed shut, but through the screen we could see a long-handled pump and a trough on the porch. "Do you reckon it works?" Quentin said. I couldn't tell if there was water in the trough or not. We knocked on the door and yelled, but nobody answered. Wind had picked up more and whined in the eaves. Gulls screamed in the air overhead.

Quentin looked into the building that appeared to be a garage and found a tire iron. With the flat end he pried open the screen door, and I rushed in and grabbed the pump handle, raised the arm and pushed down, then lifted it again. There was a groan in the pipe below, and at first I thought the well must be dry. But I pushed the handle again and again and heard a kind of gurgle in the pipe and then a sneeze, and water coughed out of the spigot. I put my head down and drank and let water run across my cheek and around my neck.

The water had a funny taste, a little like iron, somewhat like baking soda. But I was so thirsty it tasted wonderful all the same. I stood back and pumped while Quentin drank, and saw we were lucky to find the house and a well that wasn't dry.

Soon as we gulped our fill we started looking for something to put water in, for we'd need to carry some with us. We had to keep moving north, and we might not find another well for a long time. There was a bucket beside the trough and a tub on the floor, but we couldn't carry water very far in either. I looked through cracks between boards into the kitchen and saw glasses and dishes on a counter. I scanned for a jug or big jar with a lid.

"Hey, look here," Quentin said. In the corner of the porch sat a jug about a third full. I unscrewed the lid and sniffed: vinegar. I poured the vinegar into the trough. It took four rinsings to get the smell out of the jug, but when it was clean I filled it with water and twisted on the lid. Just as I finished wiping the outside of the jug we heard a tut-tut-tut noise from the beach, like a car coming across the sand. Quentin ran outside and looked around the corner of the house, then slipped back into the screened porch.

"It's a police car and they've stopped," he said.

Too late for us to run into the dunes or hide in the garage. A car door slammed and voices approached the house. I looked around for some place to hide. The trough was not big enough to conceal us. There was a piece of canvas in the corner of the porch with streaks of paint on the fabric, like somebody had used it for a drop-cloth. I pointed to the tarpaulin, and quick as we could we unfolded the heavy cloth and crawled under it. Just as I was about to cover my head I grabbed our bag of supplies by the door.

The cops must have driven miles along the beach and they seemed in a hurry. They pounded on the front door and then walked around the back.

"Ain't nobody here," one said.

"Nobody with any sense would stay," the other said.

"Them boys are long gone," the first one said.

I heard one of the cops pissing in the sand by the porch screen.

"Let's get back to town," the other said.

Quentin and I lay still under the hot, smelly canvas.

"These winter people expect us to look after their damned houses," the first cop said as they walked away. Soon as we heard the car leave we flung the canvas aside and dusted ourselves off.

"They're looking for us," Quentin said.

"Tell me about it," I said. I pumped more water and took a deep drink, and Quentin drank again too.

"I'll bet there's something to eat in the house," Quentin said.

"We've got stuff to eat."

Quentin found a hammer in the garage and nailed the screen door shut again. If somebody looked close they'd see the screen door had been forced, but it wasn't obvious. When we got back to the beach we followed the car tracks to the north. The tide was coming in and the beach wasn't as wide as before. Birds trotted along the front of the waves, and soon waves washed over the tire tracks. I lugged the heavy jug, and Quentin toted the bag of grub and fishing tackle.

The wind had picked up more, coming from the south and combing sand off the beach so it stung my ankles and peppered my pants. The sky grew cloudy and I noticed the waves were bigger and frothier, and they stretched further before they crashed. The ocean looked like lather churned up and whipped, and higher waves swept in and rode over the top of other waves, and slid long tongues of spit right to our feet.

The air felt even stranger, like it had grown thin and was about to disappear, or leak out of itself. The air felt like it had sparks in it and might catch fire. And then wind pushed against my back like it was trying to shove me down.

"Do you think it's going to rain?" I said.

Wind picked up faster and faster up the beach, like a big hand that pushed me every time I took a step. There was a new strength in the blast.

"I hope this ain't a hurricane, like you hear about," Quentin said.

"Don't see any storm clouds," I said. I'd heard of hurricanes and seen pictures in the paper of wrecked houses and knocked-down trees. They roared right up the coast to North Carolina. But hurricanes came in late summer and fall.

"Too early in the season for a hurricane," I said.

Quentin reminded me it was July, plenty late for a hurricane. I remembered that the man in the store had said there was weather coming. But I didn't see how you could have a hurricane without dark storm clouds. Sun still splashed through the clouds and flashed on the waves. But when I looked behind I did see clouds stacked up, and far to the south dark thunderheads gnashing and fighting among themselves, and tearing apart like they were having fits. I'd never seen clouds boil so high and crazy.

"Maybe it's just a storm and not a hurricane," Quentin said.

The ocean leapt higher and foamier. Waves climbed on the backs of waves and leapfrogged each other. Waves slid like cutter bars mowing all the little waves in front of them. Waves flung down on the sand like boys diving into water.

"If there's going to be a storm we'd better find a house," I said.

Quentin said we'd come to another house soon, if we kept walking.

"It'll be all boarded up," I said.

"We can tear away the boards."

With wind pushing us we took longer steps, walking faster to keep from falling. The wind nudged and rammed so hard my shirt felt glued to my back. And then the wind swung around and hit from the ocean, pressing the side of my face so hard I couldn't think. Quentin held the bag to his chest with both hands around it. The jug of water swung in the wind and I swapped it from one hand to the other.

I reckon we must have walked four or five miles, but still didn't see a house. We kept an eye out for another patrol car, but never saw one. It was like we were the only people left in the whole world. We came to a place where a tidal creek emptied into the ocean and waded through mud and sand up to our knees.

"Ain't any more houses," Quentin said.

Spray flung off waves so thick it looked like smoke. Spray pecked and peppered the side of my face.

"What is that?" I hollered and pointed to what looked like a roof farther up the beach. In the mist of spray it was hard to be sure. We started stepping faster, but had to walk in soft sand because the waves came across the firm sand and lunged up against the dunes. We walked through thick grass as waves tossed arms that got smacked to pieces in the wind. The jug banged against my leg and grew heavier and heavier. The house we'd seen before was hidden by spray, but when it appeared again it seemed no closer.

"Can a house run away from us?" I shouted.

A big wave drove in on my right and lashed spray against my arm and cheek. The wind pushed so hard drops stung like birdshot. I dropped to my knees in the sand, and then stumbled ahead. Quentin fell and a can of pork and beans rolled out of the bag and disappeared in the grass. We let it go. The wind pounded the dunes and kept pushing us to the left. Every time I took a step I was knocked sideways. To keep in a straight line I had to walk at an angle.

"We've got to get away from the ocean," I said.

"We're getting closer," Quentin said and pointed to the house ahead.

If a bad storm came, people were supposed to flee inland, to get away from the worst fury, more dangerous beside the ocean. Land slowed a storm down and wore it out. That's why the mountains usually didn't have bad hurricanes.

"We've got to get away from the beach," I hollered.

Quentin pointed toward the house ahead. "Maybe if we lay low this will blow over."

The wind was stripping the beach and dunes. Sand flew in sheets of razor-sharp grains. Wind peeled the dunes of flaking, sharp pieces that burned my ankles and stung through my britches' legs. There was nothing to do but wrestle against the wind toward the house. Spray and sand shot right into my nose and eyes and mouth. I spit out salty sand and wiped my lips with the back of my fist. I kept my eyes closed as much as I could. As we stomped and stumbled across the dunes there was a flash of lightning and thunder broke out of the sky behind our heads. The sun was gone and it was getting darker. Thunder was drowned in the roar of the ocean and wind.

It was a little house built on stilts or pilings. There was a deck with railing and stairs going up to the deck. But the house was boarded up tight as the one where we got the water. Every window and door had planks nailed over it. We stumbled around the back and found everything there nailed shut.

"I can find something to pry a plank loose," Quentin shouted.

"We don't have time!" I yelled. Even if we could break into the house it was a dangerous place. Big waves could wash the little house away. We needed to hunker down in a ditch as far inland as possible.

"Are you scared?" Quentin hollered. He pounded on the railing of the stairs.

"Damn right I'm scared."

"Then run away, you sissy!" Quentin shouted. It was like the wind had made him crazy, as if the storm was attacking him personally. I understood that the wind was so strong you felt insulted, with sand and spray flung in your face. But Quentin acted like he wanted to pick a fight with the storm, or with me, like the storm might back down if he was angry enough.

"We've got to get away from here!" I shouted.

"Ain't running away," Quentin said. It was the same stubbornness he'd shown trying to organize the union among the road crew. Just then there was more thunder, and a terrible ripping came out of the sky, sounding like the sky itself was tearing open. I looked up and witnessed the whole roof tilt up and twist away.

"Look out!" I screamed and jumped aside. A section of the roof fell away from the house and got swatted over the dunes, jumping and cartwheeling like a piece of cardboard. That told me how awful the wind was, and when I took another step I felt new force in the air. Sand burned my face and I had to put a hand over my eyes and turn away from the brunt to face inland. I stumbled and was knocked down, then crawled over a dune, dragging the jug of water behind me.

There was a kind of road over the dunes and I stooped low as I could to follow the tracks through tall grass flattened by wind. Quentin staggered behind me and

wind hit us both like a big fist. I didn't look back. I was
trying to stay upright and keep my head low. Shingles
hurled past, and pieces of wood. A window frame went
wheeling and leaping over the sand. I figured the house
behind was being jerked apart, piece by piece. I was hit
in the back by a mop handle. When I fell Quentin fell
against me. My shirt was pulled out of my pants and
the tail jerked up over my head. The shirt was pulled
against my armpits, and sand stung my back.

The wind near the beach had been strong enough to
knock us down, but that was nothing compared to the
force that slammed us from behind as we staggered
and stumbled farther into the woods. The air behind
was a wall that pushed like a bulldozer blade. The sky
roared so close I couldn't hear my own thoughts as I
fell forward still holding the jug and Quentin gripped
my belt. Rabbits and birds went tumbling along the
ground.

I tried to stand up taller, but got knocked right down.
Quentin said something but I couldn't tell what it was.
I crawled along the track and wind pushed me over on
my face and I got a mouthful of sand.

"Whoa!" I screamed like I expected somebody to
turn off the wind.

Quentin slammed against me and I heard him say,
"Oh, Jesus." I reckon he was praying. And I tried to
pray too. I prayed that if I'd done a lot of bad things
like running away from home, and tying up the deputy,
I would be forgiven. I prayed that a tree wouldn't fall
and smash us. I prayed that we'd survive and get back
to the highway, and catch a ride home. It was past time
for me to be back home.

The rain was so loud my mind was all a mess, and
rain drops flew by like bullets from a battle and stung my
face and neck. Lightning bleached the air and woods, but
wind was now so loud I didn't hear thunder anymore.
I crawled forward on my knees and elbows and was

pushed down and rolled over. A plank slammed against a tree and then went tumbling again end over end.

And then we fell into a kind of hole, like a pit that had been hollowed out, where sand had been dug. Sticks and leaves and pieces of trash lay on the bottom, but the wind was not so awful there. I pushed myself into the lowest part and found a snake among the litter, just a few inches from my face. I tried to jerk away but Quentin was jammed against me. I couldn't back away and I couldn't go forward. And I couldn't stand up in the deadly blast. With my free hand I grabbed the snake and hurled it as far as I could. I thought it was a copperhead, but couldn't be sure.

All the wind that had come before seemed like a breeze compared to what hit us now. The air pressed into my face so hard I thought it was going to break my skin and nose. I lay flat on the ground and worked my elbows into the sand. I pushed my face against the ground and felt wind tear and claw at my clothes and hair.

There was something ancient and awful about the warm blizzard. It was like something I'd heard about long ago and forgot. It was a howling from the beginning of the world, a scream from the stars and the start of time, the howl of insanity and worlds breaking apart. The storm roared with blasphemy, and ten million freight trains going over our heads. It was the authentic noise of chaos, of creation, and the pain of birth, the cruelty and heartbreak of people's lives. I buried my face in sand and closed my eyes, for it seemed I heard the voice of hell itself, the lake of fire, and eternal damnation. And then I thought, yes, maybe this is the true voice of God and His wrath shouted down the hallways and lunatic corridors of time.

Sticks and leaves and little animals fell on top of us. Rain soaked the floor of the hole, and I felt water and bugs of all kinds swirling and crawling and scratching over me. But I didn't pay them much mind. The wind was so fast it seemed to make time stop and run backwards. It was the roar of a fiery furnace. The world had started in fire, one of my schoolteachers had said. Or maybe the wind was so powerful it was rushing us ahead of time, speeding up toward the end of time the preachers talked about. I clutched the sand like I was afraid of being snatched away, and I waited and waited and rain soaked me and made a puddle around my face.

I don't know when I realized the air had slacked. I was so used to the roar I reckon I was still hearing it long after it had stopped. I held onto the wet sand hoping not to be sucked out of the ditch, and then slowly noticed the storm had quieted. Limbs and flying things no longer hit me. Rain sprinkled and pecked my back and tickled my neck and ears. The air was not pushing or clawing at me.

I raised my head and my face was not smacked down. Opened my eyes and saw the light had grown brighter. Where there had been woods before was nothing but knocked-down trees. I looked over the rim of the hole. A few bushes stood in pools of water, but all around them was a mess of twisted trunks and limbs. A piece of what looked like a dock or pier tilted sideways in the sand. Far as I could see there wasn't a thing but broken-down trees and tangled vines and brush. It was a different world from what had been there earlier.

Quentin lay just as quiet as he had before. I guess he thought the gale was still pounding us. "Get up!" I hollered and nudged him with my foot. Quentin raised his head all covered with sand and twigs and leaves, then brushed off his cheek and looked around. "It's the eye of the storm," he said.

"What do you mean?"

Quentin said hurricanes were just big circles of wind. He'd seen a picture of a hurricane in a newspaper. At the center was a calm spot, but when that passed over the storm would hit again, with wind coming from the opposite direction. It would feel like the storm passed on and then came back. The lull would last only a few minutes.

I thought I heard a voice yell, "Help!" Quentin heard it too, for he turned and I caught the surprise on his face as he looked past me. I whirled to find what had startled him, and saw a big boat leaning crazy in the mess of brush and twisted trees. It was a long boat, nearly as tall as a house, with windows and railing around the deck. The front of the boat looked like it had been smashed against a tree.

"Help me!" someone called again.

We stumbled out of the hole and started toward the cabin cruiser. The boat was tilted so far it looked like it might roll on over, except it was lodged on broken-down trees. It was hard to believe that a boat that big had been pushed by wind and waves this far from the ocean. The cruiser sat on the tangled mess that had once been the woods.

"Help!" we heard again from inside the boat. It was a woman's voice. It had been a fine boat with a polished deck and shiny metal fittings. But limbs and leaves and dirt were strewn all over the deck. A dead bird was caught on the rail. Painted on the side in black letters was the name "Tinkerbell."

"Here!" the voice yelled again.

The boat was tilted so far over I could reach and grab the railing and pull myself up on the deck where I saw steps going down inside. Above was a higher deck with a windshield, helm, and control panel with dials and levers.

"Where are you?" I yelled.

"In here," the voice answered.

I eased down the steps, rocking the boat a little every time I moved. I reckon the craft was just barely balanced on the logs and limbs it was lodged against. So dark inside I couldn't see anything but spilled clothes and fishing rods and cushions and binoculars all tangled up with leaves and trash and coils of white rope. And then I spied a shoulder, pushed down under a fallen bureau or chest of drawers.

"I can't move," the woman said, and in the dim light her long red hair and face pressed against the wet floor. There was blood on her forehead. At the angle the boat was turned it seemed impossible to plant my feet to get a purchase. I tried to lift the chest but it was too heavy. I called for Quentin and felt the boat tip as he climbed aboard. I found the woman's hand and held it.

"Where is James?" she said.

When Quentin crawled down the hatch it took both of us to lift the chest of drawers off her. She was too weak to push herself free. Quentin held the chest up while I pulled her out from under it. I dragged her free and helped her to the steps. She was a tall beautiful woman with red hair and wearing nothing but orange shorts and a kind of bandanna tied around her breasts. She was too shaky to pull herself through the hatch.

Quentin let the chest of drawers fall with a crash and the boat shuddered and rocked again. It took both of us to pull the woman up the steps and across the sloping deck to the railing. She had extra-long legs and white freckled skin, but was smeared all over with blood and dirt.

"Where is James?" she said again.

We could barely lift her over the railing and down to the ground. There was a cut in her forehead. I asked if any bones were broken and she said her left arm felt funny. The wrist on her left hand was stained with blood. Blood had run into her hair.

"I'm so thirsty," the woman said.

I tried to remember where I'd left the jug of water. It must be in the hole where we'd hidden from the storm. Climbing over brush and fallen trees to the pit, I found the jug buried in limbs, and hurried back to the woman and gave her a drink.

"You have saved my life," she said. She said her name was Delores Shealy, and that we must look for her husband.

"Is your husband on the boat?" I asked.

She said she didn't know. He was on the deck the last time she'd seen him, trying to steer the boat toward shore. But in the high wind she'd been blinded by spray, and then a wave higher than a mountain roared over the boat and tumbled it around and around. When it came to rest she was lying in the hold with the chest of drawers on top of her and pain in her arm.

"You must look for James," she said. "He's not worth anything, but he's my husband."

I took off my shirt and folded it and put it under her head for a pillow. And then I climbed back into the boat and down into the hold. It was so dark inside I had to feel my way among the clothes and pillows and fishing rods. I touched something soft, but it was just a stuffed animal. I banged my head on the leg of an overturned table, and stuck my hand in something sticky, like spilled oil or syrup. "James!" I called, then had to crawl back out and tell her there was nobody in the wrecked boat.

"Then look in the woods, god damn it!" she snapped.

I reckoned the woman was in shock; the lick on her head must have addled her. "My name is Delores Shealy," she said again. "And you must look for my husband."

I asked her where she thought we should look. She started, like she'd just remembered something. "My husband will make it worth your while," she said.

I looked around the cabin cruiser in the great tangled mess of broken trees and all kinds of litter. There were bottles and cans, pieces of rope, and furniture among the clutter. I found a wadded-up shirt, but there was no body. I pulled a piece of picket fence away and spotted a dead dog. If her husband had been swept overboard he was almost certainly out in the ocean, or he could have been washed ashore miles away. I looked again in the brush behind the boat but didn't find anything.

Quentin came up behind me and said in a low voice, "What are we going to do with her before the other side of the storm hits?"

I'd forgotten we were in the lull. The hurricane was only half finished and us far from any shelter and safety. I had no idea how far it was to a highway. The woman named Delores was injured and we had no place to protect her. I circled back to where Delores lay on the ground still looking dazed and told her James might be farther down the coast, or up the coast. Or he might have been washed farther inland.

"We've got to find him," she said.

I told her the storm would return any minute, that this was just the eye.

"No!" she said. "I'll walk into the woods looking for James." She stood up but was so unsteady I had to hold her on one side and Quentin grabbed her on the other.

"Call on the radio," she said, like she'd just remembered the radio. She said the radio was on the deck beside the steering wheel or helm. If I could call the Coast Guard somebody would come. We led her back to the boat and I climbed up on the railing so I could reach the instrument panel. I pressed the knob she pointed to and screeches and whistles blasted out of the box. A light shone behind a dial and needles flickered.

"Push down the bar and shout "Mayday! Mayday!" Delores said.

I pressed down the bar and hollered "Mayday! Mayday!" then said it again three times.

"Release the bar," Delores called, and I did.

"Identify yourself," a voice said from the panel. I was so surprised I couldn't think what to say.

"The Tinkerbell," Delores shouted. "This is the Tinkerbell."

"What is your location?" the voice said after I told him it was the Tinkerbell. "We're on land about twenty miles north of Drum," I said.

"I'll contact the state police," the voice said. "But I'm sure they're already overwhelmed with calls."

"Call my husband!" Delores yelled.

The rain started again and wind picked up. But now the wind came from inland and blowing back toward the ocean. I saw that would be the way if the storm was moving in a circle. Most of the mess blown in from the shore would be swept out again. Broken trees would be knocked around and driven away.

Wind stiffened and the sky darkened. Wind shoved my face, smelling of raw wood and mud and rotten things.

"We've got to hide from the wind," I said to Delores, but she was too confused to understand. She was truly in shock. I climbed back into the boat and reached into the hold to gather all the blankets and raincoats and jackets I could find. We put a raincoat around Delores's beautiful shoulders and led her toward the hole where we'd hid before.

The wind was now so bad we had to stoop, facing daggers of air, and one of the blankets ripped from my grasp and shot away. "Whoa!" I called.

The pit where we'd lain before had leaves and limbs and papers and water in it.

"I won't lie down in that mess," Delores said.

"We've got no other place to go," Quentin said.

We pushed her down into the pit just as the wind seared more terrible. Brush and sand and leaves and all kinds of trash flew into my face. I slipped on a raincoat and Quentin put one on too.

"I want to look for James," Delores said, but a wad of leaves and moss lodged in her mouth and she gagged and spat. Lightning flashed like a thousand photographer's flashes, and then sticks and dirt and sticky things hit us like they'd been fired out of a cannon. I tried to wrap a blanket around the three of us, but the blanket jerked away and we had to duck below the rim of the hole. It had grown dark.

"Don't raise your head or you'll be killed by a flying limb," I said to Delores.

"We have to look for James," she said again.

The wind had teeth like broken glass. It howled with
a madness from somewhere deep before the beginning of
meaning. Wind pawed at us in the hole. The roar of the
wind was like a message too awful to think about. The
scream of the storm came out of the sky and from all
around and from deep in the ground and echoed inside
my head from before memory. Delores tried to rise out
of the hole. Thunder blasted like dynamite just a few feet
away and she dropped back down. I put my arm over
her to hold her down. She was smeared with dirt and
blood, but she was still the prettiest woman I'd ever seen.

"We'll look for James when the storm's over," I
promised.

The wind that came now was the kind that could
strip bark off trees. The ground shook like a million
bulldozers were running over it. The air was sharp with
cutting sand. The wind sounded like it was coming right
out of Hades. There was a shriek that hurt the marrow
in my bones and the pressure in my guts. I thought: this
is the howl of being born, and the terror of pain, and
death. It's the scream a newborn baby knows, and that
the dying remember. The wind pulled and jerked us as
we lay in the bottom of the hole, as we tried to hold
onto each other and onto the sand. The air had insanity
pushing us, trying to shove us into a white-hot furnace.

Delores was talking and at first I couldn't tell what
she said. And then I understood she was praying, or
trying to pray. She was reciting a Psalm: "Yea, though
I walk through the valley of the shadow of death, I will
fear no evil." She was crying too.

I saw that if the wind raked us out of the hole we'd
be bashed against logs. We'd be tumbled and slammed
against sand dunes and maybe flung into the ocean.
There was nothing to do but pray and push our faces
down in the sand and water. We'd done all we could
and were helpless. Something heavy rolled against me.
It felt like a two-hundred-pound bag of fertilizer that
slammed against my shoulder. I turned to see what was

crushing me, and in the flare of lightning I found black fur and a long snout. It was a bear that had rolled into the pit, and I could smell its stink.

I didn't holler out. Maybe I didn't want to scare the others, or maybe I was too surprised and scared to yell. The bear pressed against me and struggled to get up. I guess it was as scared of me as I was of it. The beast raised up and then was swept away from the hole. I reckon the bruin went tumbling and rolling like everything else in the deadly wind.

Suddenly I felt I couldn't take any more of the storm. It had gone on too long. I found myself howling back at the wind, the way boys sometimes bark at a mean dog. Something in me had to answer the dogs of madness, the hounds of war, the rage of the storm, with a deep howl of my own despair. I found myself growling in my throat, bellowing and growling. I was growling at the deputy that hit me with the chain, and the boss who had fired us. I was answering the ravings of the sky and the elements, the cruelty of the Depression.

And when I paused to get my breath I heard Quentin howling too, and then Delores bellowing and screaming by turns. She'd quit praying and was screaming defiance at the storm. The hounds of hell had been turned loose and bore down on us, and we answered them with our own baying, whether defiant or hopeless I couldn't say. I'd never spoken in growls and howls before. The sounds came from deep in my throat and bowels and marrow and far back in my brain.

When the wind finally slacked, rain fell even harder. It was a steady summer rain on broken trees and stumps. The boat had rolled away, maybe all the way back to the ocean, for it was nowhere in sight.

"Oh my God," Delores said, "where is James?"

"James wasn't on the boat," I said. "I looked"

Quentin said her husband might have come ashore farther up the coast.

"He may be looking for you right now," I said.

We stood in the rain trying to think what to do, and then I picked my way to where the little road had been. Trees and limbs covered the tracks and the ruts had mostly been washed away. Delores and Quentin followed me. The road was so cluttered it was almost impossible to follow. I climbed around stumps and over logs. Deep pools filled low spots and rain made goose bumps on the water.

"Do you have a car?" Delores said.

I told her we'd been hitch-hiking. If we could get to the highway we might hitch a ride. I didn't explain we were trying to avoid the sheriff. I took my raincoat off and put it on her shoulders. Her own coat must have been lost in the wind. Because the woods had been knocked down and churned up, it was hard to tell what direction to turn. Though I could still hear the roar of the ocean, we'd come too far inland to see the dunes. It was almost impossible to follow the track under the tangles of limbs and wide pools. I thought I spotted a stretch of the trail here and a piece farther on.

We led Delores between the stumps and heaps of limbs and vines. A snake lay stunned in the sand. I prodded it with a stick and it coiled like a spring. The rattles on its tail buzzed. Delores screamed and pulled back. Quentin picked up a stick and hit the snake on the head and then flung the flopping body off into brush. I listened for cars on a highway, but all I heard was the typing of rain on leaves and the faraway roar of the ocean.

I asked Delores where she lived. "Our house is in Fort Pierce," she said. "But we keep our boat at the marina at St. Lucie."

Quentin asked if there might be somebody at home to answer if we could find a telephone. She said the cook might be there, and the chauffeur. Watching for more snakes as I led her through the crazy maze, I saw a dead rabbit and a lot of dead birds. It seemed the ground had already started to stink with rotten things. Maybe it was just mud and torn-out roots, but I could smell worse too. And then I saw what was stinking. I'd almost stepped into the hole before seeing the turned-over outhouse among the sticks and vines. The toilet had been toppled by wind and I'd almost fallen in the pit of soil and toilet paper. The house nearby was a little one-story building. It had been turned around on its foundation and the roof was crushed.

"Maybe this house will have a telephone," Delores said.

Wires drooped from a pole beside the house, but I couldn't tell if they were electric wires or telephone wires. The windows and doors of the house had planks nailed over them, but the boards had come loose over one window and the glass was broken. I raised the lower half of the window and looked inside. It was dark in the room and chairs and rugs, rags and pictures, were scattered and toppled. Water stood a foot deep on the floor. The house smelled of sour rags that had lain in a hot dark place.

"See if there's a telephone," Delores called.

I crawled through the window and stepped carefully among the clutter of glass shards in standing water. If there was a telephone it would have fallen in the water and the cord would be severed. The ceiling was cracked and the doorway to the kitchen shattered. An icebox had tipped over, and jars and bottles, busted eggs and dirty carrots floated in the water on the floor. I was ready to leave, but decided to look in the bedroom, which was in the half of the house where the roof had caved in. The door to the bedroom had been ripped off its hinges, but it was too dark to see much. The ceiling had come down on the bed and a beam had pushed through the ceiling. In the dim light I tried to see where the timber had stuck in the bed.

"Is there a telephone?" Delores yelled from the window.

As I glanced around I glimpsed in the corner of my eye what was in the bed: an old man with his mouth open like he was yelling. But he was still. The beam had gone right through his chest and into his heart like a giant spear thrown from heaven. I listened for his breathing, but the only sound was rain on the roof. I backed away and sloshed to the living room window.

"Is there a telephone?" Delores called again. I decided not to tell her and Quentin about the man. We couldn't help the old fellow, and it wouldn't do any good for them to know about his ill luck. I wished I hadn't seen the man's open eyes and his mouth stretched in a scream. When I climbed back out the window I told Delores I doubted any telephone would be working now, even if we could find one. Because of the storm, all lines would be down and there wouldn't be electricity to carry messages.

"If we get to the highway we can hitch-hike, ma'am," Quentin said.

Delores said, "Maybe the police will come along and help us look for James."

Now that the storm had passed, there was just rain, with little gusts. James must have been knocked overboard in the high wind. It would be a miracle if he'd survived, clinging to a tree, or been washed onto higher ground.

"We'll help you look for James," I said.

"You've been so kind," Delores said. Her forehead had quit bleeding, but she was still a little dazed.

We worked our way through scrub and twisted brush. The tracks went under water for maybe a quarter of a mile, and we had to wade, watching for snakes threading through the floating mess. A turtle the size of a dishpan sat on a log. Dead birds floated in the flood water. We passed another house that had been smashed like a giant had stepped on the roof and walls. There was no use to look inside for a telephone, for all the wires into the house had broken. I wondered if we could be electrocuted, walking in water where the powerlines had fallen.

The rain kept splattering and it was starting to get

dark. I'd hoped we'd find the highway before it was really dark, for Delores was hurt and groggy and there seemed no place to stop, no shelter out of the rain. We couldn't just leave her, and besides, we had no place to go ourselves. We climbed over more logs and waded through more puddles. The rain seemed endless. The sour of the dying leaves and weeds and rotten things filled the air. In the high wind, Quentin had lost the bag with our cans of beans and sardines. I couldn't remember where the water jug was. I wondered if we could find a house where there was anything to eat. I wasn't sure our matches would strike, even if Quentin still had the matches.

And then, as the rain splashed harder and the twilight turned to darkness, we stumbled onto the highway. I wasn't sure at first what it was. My feet touched a bed of concrete, and I thought it might be the floor of a building that had blown away. And then I spied the white line in the middle. The poles of the telegraph line had been knocked over.

"It's the coastal highway," Quentin said.

"Oh, my God," Delores said.

There was no traffic. Brush lay in the road and tips of downed trees reached halfway across the lanes. Quentin and I needed to head north, but I wasn't sure where Delores should go. She said her house was in Fort Pierce, but I didn't know where that was. She probably needed to get to a doctor or hospital. She had to find a shelter out of the rain, and we had to get her off our hands. And we had to avoid the police until we got farther from the Everglades.

"Which way is your house?" I said.

She pointed north and said, "We have to look for James."

"James may already have reached home or called home," I said, though pretty sure he hadn't done either.

Just then we noticed headlights coming from the north. It was startling to see two bright beams cutting through the rain and brush, two big yellow lights. The

headlights approached slowly, turning this way and
that, weaving between downed trees. They stopped and
then went around brush and poles and other trash on
the road. The lights looked awfully big. I wondered if it
was a police car, if Quentin and I should jump into the
brush and start running. I wondered if the driver had
already seen us. And then I saw it was a Packard, likely
driven by a chauffeur.

"The car will stop and help you," I said to Delores.

"You're not going to leave me?" she said.

I told her we'd stay with her until she was safe. We
couldn't just run away and abandon her standing by the
road. We'd have to hope the driver didn't recognize us.
The car wove from one side of the highway to the other,
dodging brush and logs and dead animals. I stepped
out in the middle of the road and waved and the big
car stopped. Quentin and Delores and I stood in the
blinding glare of the headlights. I feared to hear a voice
yell that I was under arrest. The driver's door opened
and a voice called out, "Miz Shealy, is that you?"

"Is that you, Adger?" Delores screamed, and a sob
broke from her throat. She stepped forward and fell
and I helped her up.

"It's Adger, the chauffeur," she said.

"Miz Shealy, you've been hurt," Adger said. "Coast
Guard called and said you landed down here." He was
a tall black man in a uniform and he walked toward us.

"You've got to look for James," Delores said. "And
we must help these boys who saved me."

"Whatever you say, Miz Shealy," the chauffeur said,
and looked at us up and down in our rags and dirt.

"Is there a railroad near your house?" Quentin said.

"About a mile away" Delores said.

"Then we'll ride with you that far," Quentin said.

ACKNOWLEDGMENTS

I would like to thank Jesse Graves and Randall Wilhelm for their inspiring response as first readers of these stories, and Kevin Morgan Watson for his laser-like eye as editor. Thanks also to Paul Sawyer, J. Robert Lennon, Cynthia Chase, and the late Michael Koch.

"Beyond the Outer Banks" first appeared in a different
  version in *Appalachian Heritage*
"Devil's Courthouse" and "Judaculla Rock" first
  appeared in *Epoch*

Robert Morgan is the author of several books of poems, including *Terroir* (2011) and *Dark Energy* (2015). He has published ten books of fiction, including *The New York Times* bestseller *Gap Creek*, and, most recently, *Chasing the North Star* (2016) and *As Rain Turns to Snow* (2017). His works of nonfiction include *Lions of the West* (2011), and the national bestseller *Boone: A Biography* (2007). Recipient of awards from the Guggenheim Foundation and the American Academy of Arts and Letters, he is currently Kappa Alpha Professor of English (Emeritus) at Cornell University.